DOCTOR
AND SON

BY
MAGGIE KINGSLEY

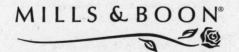

MILLS & BOON®

First published in Great Britain 2002
Harlequin Mills & Boon Limited,
Eton House, 18-24 Paradise Road, Richmond, Surrey TW9 1SR

© Maggie Kingsley 2002

ISBN 0 263 83419 0

Set in Times Roman 10½ on 11¼ pt.
03-0103-51160

Printed and bound in Spain
by Litografía Rosés, S.A., Barcelona

What in the world was happening to him? Gideon wondered.

Just four short weeks ago his life had been ordered, settled. He'd had his work, his career, and that was all he'd wanted, and then a golden-haired girl with large blue eyes had cannoned into him on the hospital staircase, torn his character to shreds, and nothing had been the same.

Because you're falling in love with her, a little voice whispered at the back of his mind. He crushed the voice down quickly. It wasn't true—couldn't be true. He liked his life the way it was. No emotional entanglements, no potential for heartache, and yet...

She was blowing on Jamie's chips to cool them, and all he could think was how wonderful it would be to turn her head, to capture those lips with his own and taste them.

Sex, he told himself firmly. These thoughts—these feelings—they don't mean anything except that your hormones have kicked into life.

But it wasn't just sex, he realised with dismay when Annie laughed at something Jamie had said, then turned to him to share the joke. Yes, he wanted to hold her, to touch her, but he also knew that he never wanted to let her go.

THE BABY DOCTORS

The gynaecology department at the Belfield Infirmary, Glasgow, is a very special place, and it employs a very special team of people. Doctors who are all dedicated to helping patients fulfil their dreams for a family by helping them bring babies safely into the world. Some of these doctors have families of their own; some are still searching. Some of them are married to each other; some of them are meant for each other. But, whatever their personal problems, they are all committed to giving their patients the best chance of a child.

**For THE BABY DOCTORS—
making families is their business.**

We hope you enjoy Gideon and Annie's story in DOCTOR AND SON. Look out for the next two books in this emotional trilogy from Maggie Kingsley, where you can read about the conflicted marriage of Dr Tom Brooke and Dr Helen Fraser, and see if the charms of outsider David Hart work on the spiky Special Registrar Rachel Dunwoody.

Medical Romance™...medical drama on the pulse

CHAPTER ONE

ANNIE was going to be late. Very late.

'Take the lift to the fifth floor,' the porter had said. 'Turn right when you get out, then left, then right again, and Obs and Gynae is through the double doors at the end of the corridor.'

It had sounded so easy—so simple—and it probably would have been if the Belfield Infirmary's ancient elevator buttons had been working properly, and if what they'd proclaimed to be the fifth floor hadn't, in fact, turned out to be the third.

I am *not* going to cry, Annie told herself as she hurried down yet another of the Belfield's rambling Victorian corridors in a desperate search for the stairs. Grown-up women of twenty-eight didn't cry. Jamie hadn't cried this morning when she'd left him at the day-care centre, and he was only four.

'You will remember to come back for me, Mummy?' was all he'd said, his blue eyes huge in his little face, his small nose reddened by the cold January wind. 'You won't forget?'

And she'd been the one who'd got all choked up, and now she was on the verge of tears all over again because she was late. Late for the first job she'd had since Jamie was born, and if she messed it up she was never going to get another one.

'It's full time, you know, Dr Hart,' the head of administration at the Belfield Infirmary had said, gazing at her uncertainly. 'And your shifts won't always be eight until four. There may be some night work, some afternoon shifts… Look, I guess what I'm trying to say is, you have a young child. Are you sure you're up to it?'

And Annie had said of course she was up to it—had even gone out and bought two of the most modern medical manuals to make doubly sure she was up to it—and now everything had gone wrong, and she hadn't even started.

'Whoa, there, where's the fire?' a deep male voice protested as she raced out of the door marked STAIRS and cannoned straight into him.

'I'm sorry—so sorry,' she gasped, temporarily winded. 'But I should have been in Obstetrics and Gynaecology ten minutes ago, and—'

'Hey, calm down,' the man interrupted, amusement plain in his voice. 'So you're late. It's hardly a hanging offence, is it?'

Which was all very well for him to say, she decided, prising her nose out of his rough tweed jacket and looking up. Nothing and no one would ever frighten this man. He was big—seriously big. OK, so at five feet six she wasn't exactly a giant herself, but this man had to be six feet five at least.

'Please—you'll have to excuse me,' she exclaimed, trying to sidestep him without success, 'but it's my first day on the ward, and I'm supposed to report to a Dr Dunwoody—'

'You *work* in Obs and Gynae?' he interrupted, his forehead pleating into a sudden frown.

'As from today I do.' She nodded. 'I'm the department's new junior doctor.'

'Oh, I see.' His frown cleared. 'Well, I wouldn't worry too much about Woody. She might seem a bit brusque on the surface, but underneath she's a real pussy cat.'

Yeah, right, Annie thought with a sinking heart. In her experience people described as pussy cats invariably turned out to be tigers, and people with nicknames always did. The last specialist registrar she'd worked under had been a classic. Jet-black hair pulled back into a tight bun and a tongue which could blister paint. And Dr Dunwoody sounded exactly the same. Wonderful. Just wonderful.

'Look, you've obviously got yourself in a bit of a state so why don't I show you the way?' the man continued, as though he'd read her mind.

'No, really—there's no need,' she protested. 'Now I've found the stairs—'

'It's no trouble,' he insisted. 'As it happens, I'm going that way myself.'

Probably to visit his wife, she decided as he began taking the stairs two at a time. He wasn't wearing any hospital identification badge, but he was wearing a wedding ring, so he'd probably come in to visit his wife before he started work. He looked like the kind of man who'd do something like that. A nice man. A kind man. The sort of man you could trust.

Oh, really? her mind whispered as she hurried to catch up with him. And since when did you get to be such an expert on men? You couldn't tell a louse from a knight in shining armour four years ago so what makes you think you're any better at it now?

Because a louse would never wear such an ancient tweed jacket, or a shirt with a button missing, she argued back. He'd wear something to impress, and this man clearly didn't want—or feel the need—to impress anyone.

'It's very kind of you to help me,' she said.

He threw her a smile. 'Nonsense. The Belfield's a regular rabbits' warren, and I'd hate to think of you wandering around it for days.'

She would have done, too, she realised as she followed him through yet another door and up more stairs. The hospital she'd trained in had been brand-new, with colour-coded directions to the various departments, but the Belfield…

'Where did you do your training?' the man asked, mirroring her thoughts yet again with uncanny accuracy.

'At the Manchester Infirmary, but this is my first post since I came back to Glasgow four years ago. That's why I'm a bit nervous. Four years is a long time to be out of medicine, you see, and I'm just hoping I can cope, and...'

Why am I telling him this? she wondered, biting off the rest of what she'd been about to say. She'd made it her business ever since she'd come home not to make friends, not to let anyone get too close, and yet just because this big man was smiling down at her she was telling him things about herself. Things he had no right—or need—to know.

'Are we almost there?' she said quickly. 'Only—'

'You're late. So you keep saying.' He pushed open the door beside him and stood back. 'There you go. Obstetrics and Gynaecology.'

It was, too, and she held out her hand with relief. 'Thanks for your help. I really appreciate it.'

'Hey, rescuing damsels in distress is my speciality.' He grinned, and when her own lips curved in response he nodded approvingly. 'That's better. Now you don't look quite so much like a rabbit caught in the headlights of a car.'

'It's how I feel this morning, believe me,' she admitted, but when she tried to extricate her hand he held onto it, his face suddenly concerned.

'Look, if you have any problems with your work—want to talk to somebody about it—I'm a very good listener.'

He looked as though he would be. Not a handsome man. No way was he a handsome man. Late thirties, she guessed, with a shock of ordinary brown hair and a pair of equally unremarkable brown eyes, but he had a nice face, and an even nicer smile.

'It's kind of you to offer, but I'm sure I'll be fine,' she said.

'I mean it,' he insisted. 'Starting a new job—it's often very stressful—and if you're worried about people over-hearing us, there's lots of restaurants and pubs near the hospital where we could go and be quite private.'

Where we could be private.

A wave of disappointment coursed through her as she stared up at him. Nick had known lots of private places, too. He'd taken her to quite a few before he'd finally told her he was married but was getting a divorce. And she'd believed him. Believed every word. Well, she might have been a sap four years ago, but she wasn't a sap any more.

'I don't think so,' she said coldly, pulling her hand free.

'It would be no trouble,' the man declared. 'In fact, I'd be only too happy to help.'

Nick had said that, too, she remembered, her disap-pointment giving way to anger.

What was it with married men nowadays? Even this man she'd thought nice, kind. Just because she'd been grateful for his help he'd seen it as an invitation to some-thing else. A quiet lunch for two in some out-of-the-way restaurant. A quiet lunch he undoubtedly hoped would lead to something a whole lot more interesting.

Well, he could go take a running jump. Him with his frank, open face, tatty tweed jacket and shirt with one button missing. He could go take a running jump, pref-erably right off the top of the Kingston Bridge.

'Won't you be too busy, taking care of your wife?' she snapped.

That rattled him. She could see it from the way his jaw dropped.

'My wife?'

'Yes, your wife. Remember her—the poor woman you promised to love and to cherish? Well, I suggest you go practice your listening skills on her, mister, because this girl's not buying.'

And before he could reply she'd pushed past him and

walked through the doors marked OBSTETRICS AND GYNAECOLOGY, deliberately letting them bang shut behind her.

The nerve of the man—the sheer, unmitigated nerve. At least Nick had been smart enough to remove his wedding ring so she hadn't known he was married before she'd fallen in love with him, but this man... He wasn't simply a louse, he was stupid as well.

'Can I help you at all?'

A plump, red-headed girl wearing a sister's uniform was gazing at her curiously, and Annie managed to dredge up a smile. 'I'm Annie Hart—'

'Oh, thank goodness,' the girl exclaimed. 'Woody's been spitting nails, thinking you weren't going to show up.'

'It was the lift buttons. They said I'd reached the fifth floor—'

'Never mind about that now,' the girl interrupted. 'Just stow your gear in the staffroom and get yourself onto the ward fast. Tom and Helen are due any minute, and if Gideon arrives, too, the fat really will be in the fire. Not that he's an ogre or anything, but he's a stickler about ward rounds and we're way behind already.'

'But—'

'I'm Liz, by the way,' the girl added with a harassed smile. 'Sister Liz Baker. Welcome aboard.'

And I'm all at sea, Annie thought as the girl shot off down the corridor.

Tom—Helen—Gideon? Who were these people and, more importantly, where was the staffroom? She could see a door labelled SLUICE ROOM, another marked TOILETS—

'Dr Hart, I presume, and only twenty minutes late. I suppose I should be grateful you decided to show up at all.'

Annie's heart sank as she saw a tall, slender woman

advancing towards her. Dr Dunwoody. OK, so the hair pulled back into a tight bun was auburn instead of black, and she couldn't have been any more than thirty-five, but those cold grey eyes, the tight, pursed lips… Yup. She'd bet her first month's pay cheque this was Dr Dunwoody.

'I'm sorry I'm late, Dr Dunwoody, but—'

'Spare me the excuses, Dr Hart. All I'm interested in now you've finally got here is whether you actually know anything about medicine.'

This was a pussy cat? No way was this a pussy cat. This was a full-grown tigress, and each and every one of her claws were showing.

'Dr Dunwoody—'

'The staffroom is over there. Please, hang up your coat and get yourself out on the ward so we can see if you've been worth the wait.'

Well, hello, and welcome to Obs and Gynae, Annie thought as Dr Dunwoody strode away. It wasn't her fault the lift buttons weren't working properly. If she'd been told about them she would have got here earlier. Not that she suspected it would have made any difference. Something told her that even if she'd arrived at seven o'clock, clutching three medical degrees and a glowing reference from the BMA, Dr Dunwoody would still have hated her on sight.

There was only one thing she could do. Keep her head down, get on with her work, and maybe then Dr Dunwoody would revise her opinion of her.

It was easier said than done. By lunchtime she had a pounding headache. By mid-afternoon she felt like she'd been hit by a truck, and it wasn't the actual medicine that was the problem.

'I just feel so stupid all the time,' she told Liz Baker when they hastily grabbed a coffee in the small staffroom. 'Not knowing any of the patients—what they're in for.

Dammit, I didn't even know where the blood-pressure gauges were kept until you told me.'

'Why should you?' Liz exclaimed, munching on a chocolate biscuit with relish. 'You've only just arrived, so you can hardly be expected to immediately know everything.'

'Dr Dunwoody thinks I should.' Annie sighed. 'Dr Dunwoody thinks I'm a dork.'

'No, she doesn't. I saw the way her eyebrows shot up when you got that catheter into Mrs Ferguson in fifteen seconds flat.'

'Then why does she keep watching me?' Annie protested. 'Like she's expecting me to suddenly run amok with a kidney dish or something.'

'It's because you're a junior doctor. Look, no offence meant,' Liz continued as Annie gazed at her in surprise, 'but we've had some real corkers in the past. Junior doctors who thought it beneath their dignity to fetch a patient a glass of water. Junior female doctors who were more interested in chatting up the hospital talent than examining any patients.'

I've no intention of doing either, Annie thought grimly, only to stiffen as a familiar figure walked past the open staffroom door. It was him. Mr Mountain Man from the stairs. The big louse himself. Presumably he'd finally found time to make his duty call on his wife.

'Something wrong?' Liz asked curiously, seeing her sink further down into her seat.

Apart from never wanting to see that jerk again? Not a thing, Annie decided, but she didn't say that.

'Are there any more of those chocolate biscuits left?' she asked instead.

'Dozens. One of our ex-patients brought them in as a thank-you for Gideon, and he gave them to us.'

Gideon Caldwell, the ward consultant. She hadn't met him yet. She'd met Tom who'd turned out to be Dr

Brooke, Obs and Gynae's other specialist registrar, and his wife Helen Fraser, who was the ward SHO, but she hadn't met Mr Caldwell.

'What's he like—Mr Caldwell?' she asked.

'Lovely. Great to work for, and a terrific surgeon. Normally you'd have met him when he was doing his morning rounds, but an ectopic was brought into A and E so he's been in Theatre all morning.'

Lovely? Well, she wasn't interested in 'lovely', but 'great to work for' sounded encouraging. And she desperately needed some encouraging information after spending the better part of the day running around like a headless chicken.

Helen Fraser looked as though she could do with some upbeat news, too, judging by her harassed expression as she appeared at the staffroom door.

'No, don't get up,' she insisted when Annie scrambled hastily to her feet. 'I just wondered if either of you knew where Sylvia Renton's blood results were. I was positive I'd put them back in her file but they're not there any more.'

'Dr Brooke's got them, Dr Fraser,' Liz replied. 'He said he wasn't happy about her haemoglobin level.'

'I'm not happy about it either, which is why I wanted to check it again,' Helen said with exasperation, then smiled ruefully across at Annie. 'Men, eh? Can't live with them, can't live without them.'

I sure plan to, Annie thought, but managed an answering smile.

'Helen and Tom love each other to bits, really.' Liz chuckled when the SHO had gone. 'It's just sometimes Tom thinks he's the only doctor on the ward.'

'How long have they been married?' Annie asked, carrying her coffee cup across to the small sink.

'Ten years. They met at the Belfield when they were

both junior doctors, and have the cutest eight-year-old twins you could ever hope to meet, John and Emma.'

Jamie was cute, too, Annie thought as she followed Liz out of the staffroom. At least usually he was, but today was the first day they'd been apart since he'd been born. Please, oh, please, let him be enjoying himself, she prayed. Please, let him not be missing me. If he's unhappy and miserable, I don't know what I'm going to do. I have to work. We need the money.

'I'm sorry, what did you say?' she asked, suddenly realising that Liz was gazing at her expectantly.

'Only that I was offering you the choice of the century,' the girl replied, her lips twitching. 'Do you want me to assist when you examine Mrs Douglas, or would you prefer me to assist while you examine Mrs Gill?'

Annie stared at her suspiciously. 'I know Mrs Douglas is suffering from acute constipation after her hysterectomy. What's wrong with Mrs Gill?'

'Would you believe acute constipation, too?' Liz chuckled, and Annie laughed.

'Great choice. Actually, that reminds me of something that happened at my last hospital…'

She came to a halt. Mr Mountain Man was talking to Tom Brooke at the top of the ward. Nothing unusual about that, of course. Patients' relatives often wanted a quiet word with the specialist registrar, but it was the way Mr Mountain Man was talking to Dr Brooke. Or rather the way Tom was listening to him. Intently, deeply, almost…almost reverentially.

An awful thought crept into Annie's mind. A thought which was crazy—insane—but…

'Liz. That man talking to Dr Brooke. Who is he?'

The sister turned in the direction of her gaze and smiled. 'That's Gideon Caldwell. Our consultant.'

The man she'd met on the stairs was Obs and Gynae's *consultant*? Oh, heavens.

'Liz, Mr Caldwell's wife—she...' Annie swallowed convulsively. 'She wouldn't happen to be a patient on the ward, would she?'

'Good heavens, no. Gideon's a widower—has been for five years. Actually, it was terribly tragic. She died of ovarian cancer two years after they were married.'

Not married, but a widower. And not just a widower, but a widower whose wife had tragically died of ovarian cancer. Oh, *hell*.

'Hey, are you OK?' Liz continued, her plump face suddenly concerned. 'You've gone a really funny colour.'

Was it any wonder? Annie thought wretchedly. What must he think of her? At best that she was neurotic. At worst... She didn't even want to *think* about the worst.

Maybe he wouldn't recognise her. Maybe she'd look so different in her white coat that he wouldn't recognise her.

But he did. As he began walking down the ward, she saw him pause in mid-stride and then keep on coming. And, to her horror, Dr Dunwoody joined him.

'Annie, what's wrong?' Liz asked, looking even more worried. 'You're not going to faint, are you? Look, maybe you should sit down in the staffroom...'

The staffroom sounded good. The store cupboard sounded even better. Preferably for the next three months.

Oh, get a grip, Annie. You can hardly spend the next three months hiding in the store cupboard whenever Gideon Caldwell does his rounds. No, but she could hide in there today, and by tomorrow—OK, so it was a very long shot—by tomorrow he might have calmed down.

'I think you're right, Liz,' she said, beginning to back her way up the ward. 'I think I might just sit down for a couple of minutes.'

'OK, but— Annie, be careful.'

'It's probably just something I ate...'

'No, I mean—*Annie, watch out!*'

Too late Annie saw what the sister had been trying to tell her—that the afternoon tea trolley was right behind her. Too late she felt her hip catch it and whirled round quickly, but the damage was done. The trolley toppled over, sending its cups and saucers tumbling to the floor with a resounding crash.

For a second she stared in horror at the devastation she'd created, then turned to find Dr Dunwoody glaring at her furiously, Liz looking dumbfounded and Gideon Caldwell... Was he trying very hard not to laugh? It looked as though he was trying very hard not to laugh.

And suddenly it was all too much. The whole awful, rotten day was too much, and to her utter mortification she burst into tears.

'I'm sorry—so sorry,' she sobbed, scrabbling wildly in her pocket for a handkerchief. 'I'll get a brush and pan—clean it up...'

She didn't get a chance to. Before she could move a firm hand had grasped her by the elbow and Gideon Caldwell was propelling her out of the ward and down the corridor.

'Sir, I have to clean it up,' she protested as he steered her into his consulting room and towards a chair. 'I can't just leave—'

'One of the cleaners will do it.'

'But it was my fault,' she said, dashing a hand across her wet cheeks. 'I should—'

'Tea or coffee?' he asked, opening a cupboard and pulling out two mugs.

'Neither—I can't. Dr Dunwoody—'

'Tea or coffee—black or white—with sugar or without?'

He clearly wasn't going to take no for an answer. He equally clearly wasn't used to being refused. 'Coffee, please,' she said miserably. 'Black, no sugar.'

'Good,' he said with a nod, switching on the kettle. 'Now we're getting somewhere.'

Or merely postponing the inevitable, she thought, miserably blowing her nose. The moment when he told her his ward couldn't afford a clumsy idiot like her. The moment when he fired her. And she couldn't afford to be fired. Simply couldn't.

'Please, I know I should have been watching where I was going—but, please, won't you give me another chance? I'm not normally so clumsy, and I don't make a habit of bursting into tears—'

'I know you don't,' he interrupted, spooning some coffee into the mugs. 'The woman I met on the stairs didn't strike me as a wimp. A little strange, perhaps, but certainly not a wimp.'

Oh, cripes, he was bypassing that nightmare on the ward and going straight to her even bigger disaster on the stairs. 'Mr Caldwell—'

'The name's Gideon. I'm only Mr Caldwell in front of patients.'

She would have preferred to call him Mr Caldwell. After what she'd said to him earlier, she'd infinitely have preferred to call him Mr Caldwell.

'What I said to you on the stairs…' she said, opting out of calling him anything at all. 'I can only apologise. I made a mistake—'

'You thought I was hitting on you, didn't you?' he observed. 'You saw my wedding ring, decided my offer to help was actually a thinly disguised invitation to a future affair, and that's why you chewed my head off.'

Lord, but it sounded dreadful when he put it like that, but she couldn't deny it, much as she longed to.

'I'm sorry.'

'What interests me more is *why* you should jump to that conclusion,' he said, holding out a mug of coffee to her, then sitting down. 'I've been racking my brains off and on all day but I can't for the life of me remember saying anything which might have suggested I was some sort of sexual predator.'

Scarlet colour darkened her cheeks. 'You didn't—truly, you didn't. It was me. I was stupid—overreacted.'

Yes, but *why*? he wanted to ask. OK, so she was a very pretty girl, but surely married men weren't constantly harassing her?

Or maybe it wasn't married *men*, he suddenly thought. Maybe it was one particular married man who had put those dark shadows under her eyes, made her so thin and pale. To his surprise, the thought angered him. A lot.

Well, of course it did, he told himself. He was the head of a very busy department and if a member of his staff was having problems it was up to him to investigate before the problem affected their work. And it didn't make a blind bit of difference if the member of staff in question possessed a pair of the largest, bluest eyes he'd ever seen, and short curly hair the colour of sunripened corn. It didn't.

'And I know I shouldn't have said what I did, but if you could just give me another chance.'

The blue eyes were fixed on him, unhappy, pleading, and he gazed at her blankly. What on earth was she talking about? What second chance? And then the penny dropped.

'Good grief, Annie, I'm not going to fire you.'

'You're not?' she said faintly, and he shook his head.

'For one thing, Woody says you're an excellent doctor.'

'She does?'

'Mind you, that was before the tea trolley went west so she's probably revised her opinion by now.' He'd hoped for a chuckle. He'd hoped at the very least for a small smile, but she simply gazed at him miserably, and he frowned. 'Annie, I clearly said something to you earlier that deeply upset you, and I do wish you'd tell me what it was.'

What could she say? That it wasn't what he'd said, but the fact that she'd thought he was married that had made her so angry? He wanted her to explain, and she didn't want to explain. Her private life was just that. Private.

'I'm sorry I was so rude to you, and I'm sorry about the tea trolley,' she muttered. 'I promise it won't happen again.'

'Annie—'

'Can I go now, please?'

He stared at her in frustration. He couldn't force her to stay and drink her coffee. Couldn't hold her hostage until she told him what—or who—had caused those deep shadows under her deep blue eyes. With a sigh, he nodded.

'Just remember I'm here if you ever need someone to talk to,' he called after her as she hurried out of his consulting room. 'No strings—no hidden agenda.'

She didn't answer him—couldn't. He'd been a lot kinder to her than she deserved, but she didn't want him to be kind. She didn't want him to see her at all. She wanted anonymity. Anonymity was safe. Being noticed wasn't. She had her son, and now this job. She didn't want anything or anyone else in her life.

'Did he fire you?' Liz asked as soon as she saw her. 'I didn't think he would,' she continued with relief when Annie shook her head. 'It was an accident, and accidents can happen to anyone, can't they?'

To me more than most, Annie thought ruefully, then remembered. 'What did Dr Dunwoody say?'

Liz's eyes rolled heavenwards. 'You don't want to know.'

'As bad as that?'

'Just be grateful your shift's over.'

Annie glanced at the ward clock. Liz was right. It was almost a quarter past four. She had to go. David had offered to collect Jamie from the day-care centre and to look after him until she got home, but the last thing her brother needed was a small boy under his feet. Especially if that small boy was being difficult because he'd had a rotten day.

He hadn't. In fact, she could scarcely get a word in edgewise while Jamie excitedly told her about the toys he'd played with, the Viking longship he'd made from egg boxes and the lunch he'd enjoyed.

'I said you were worrying needlessly, didn't I?' David grinned when she finally managed to get Jamie into bed.

'I'm his mother,' she protested. 'Worrying goes with the territory.'

'I'm his uncle, and I say you worry too much.'

She did—she knew she did—just as she also knew she would never change.

'How was your day?' she asked, deliberately changing the subject.

'I didn't get the promotion.'

'Oh, David…'

'To be honest, I never really expected to. Admin and I have never really seen eye to eye, so…' He shrugged. 'It's no big deal, Annie.'

But it was. Her brother was a gifted obs and gynae specialist registrar, and if anyone deserved being made consultant at the Merkland Memorial it was him. He'd been so good to her, too. Bringing her back to Glasgow when she'd told him she was pregnant, insisting she stay with him after Jamie was born, and it hadn't been his idea for her to move out and get a place of her own.

'I can't—and I won't—live off you, David,' she'd told him when he'd protested at her decision—and had protested even more when he'd seen the flat. 'It's time I was independent.'

He'd agreed eventually, had even paid her first month's

rent, and now he hadn't got the promotion he deserved because the administration at the Merkland didn't like his innovative ideas.

'David, couldn't you—?'

'You haven't told me how you got on at the Belfield.'

Who was changing the subject now? she thought, but he clearly didn't want to talk about his own problems so obediently she told him. Told him every single, humiliating incident, and by the end, to her surprise, she was laughing about it as much as he was.

'Honestly, love, when you mess things up, you really go for it,' he exclaimed, wiping the laughter from his eyes. 'This Gideon bloke sounds all right, though. How old is he—fifty—sixty—nearing retirement?'

'Late thirties, I'd guess, but I don't see—'

'Good-looking—pot ugly? Look, just answer the question, OK?' David continued when she looked even more confused.

'Ordinary-looking, I guess, but tall—very tall—with brown hair. Well, it's more sort of beech nut brown, really,' she amended, 'with little flecks of grey at the sides. His eyes are brown, too. A kind of hazel brown—'

'Not that you noticed, of course.'

Her brother's eyes were dancing, and she gave him a very hard stare. 'David…'

'Pretty junior doctor Annie Hart arrives for her first day at work and falls headlong into the arms of tall, ordinary—but apparently not all that ordinary—consultant Gideon Caldwell. Their eyes meet across a bedpan—'

'And he hits her with it because she's the ward dork,' she finished dryly. 'David, Mr Caldwell would never be interested in me in a million years. And even if he was, I certainly wouldn't be interested in him.'

'Annie, not all obs and gynae consultants are rats,' her brother protested, 'and giving up on men because of what happened to you in Manchester is crazy. You're only twenty-eight. That's way too young to have stopped dating.'

'You date enough for both of us,' she said with a laugh, then quickly put her hand up to her brother's lips to silence him. 'David, you're my big brother, and I love you dearly, but I've got my son, and you, and now I've got a job. I don't need anything else.'

And she didn't, she thought when David went home still muttering under his breath.

She'd vowed four years ago never to let another man into her life. Never to let anyone get close enough to hurt her the way Nick had, and she'd meant it. She'd loved him so much. Believed him when he'd said he loved her. Trusted him when he'd said he was getting a divorce. And then he'd walked away, leaving her with nothing.

No, not with nothing, she thought wryly, picking up one of Jamie's toys. Jamie had been the accidental result of one of their nights of love-making, and despite everything she could never regret him.

Yes, the last four years had been tough, but things were starting to look up. Gideon Caldwell could have fired her today, and he hadn't. Jamie could have hated the day-care centre, and he'd loved it. It was going to be all right. If she could just hold onto this job, everything might finally be all right.

CHAPTER TWO

'DON'T want to go to the day centre. Want to stay home with Mummy.'

Annie glanced at the kitchen clock then back to her son's truculent face with a groan. She didn't need this, not today. Not when Gideon had asked her to sit in on his morning clinic for the very first time.

'I thought you liked the centre. You said the toys were terrific—'

'Don't want to go. Don't like it there any more.'

Annie put his cereal bowl in the sink, her brain working overtime.

'I could collect you early today,' she suggested. 'I should be finished at the hospital around two o'clock, and after I've done some quick shopping—' frantic, more like '—I could collect you at three.'

Jamie didn't look impressed. In fact, he looked even more truculent. 'I've got a sore tummy.'

'I'm not surprised considering how fast you ate your breakfast.'

'I mean a *really* sore tummy. And a sore head.'

She stared at him uncertainly. He'd been perfectly fine when he'd got up this morning, and he looked perfectly fine now, but...

'Wait here while Mummy gets her thermometer,' she ordered.

'Don't want the termoneter,' Jamie yelled after her. 'Want to stay home.'

And I'm the worst mother in the world, Annie thought when she'd taken his temperature and found it to be normal. It was obvious what was happening. The novelty of going to the centre had worn off and this was Jamie's way of telling her he felt abandoned, but what could she do? She had to work to keep a roof over their heads. She couldn't keep on relying on David for the rest of her life.

'Sweetheart, Mummy has to work—you know she does.'

'You never did when we stayed with Uncle David,' Jamie argued, his face beginning to crumple.

'Look, if you're a good boy and go to the centre, I'll buy you that pudding you like for tea,' she said swiftly. 'The one with the chocolate bits in it?'

And now I'm bribing him, she thought, seeing Jamie's face miraculously clear. Bribing my own son. But I don't have time for this. Dr Dunwoody is only just speaking to me after the tea trolley disaster on Monday, and if I'm late…

'Can I have chips for my tea, too?' Jamie asked as she helped him on with his coat. 'And beans—can I have beans with my chips?'

Beans and chips, and chocolate pudding. The hospital nutritionist would faint clean away at the sound of that diet, but if she said no she'd never get Jamie to the centre.

'OK, but only for today as a special treat,' she replied, salving her conscience. 'Now, remember—'

'Not to sing or shout going down the stairs, 'cos Mrs Patterson will come out wearing her grumpy face.'

Annie's heart constricted as she stared down at her son. He was only four. He should be able to run and play whenever he wanted, but their landlady had made her feelings only too plain when they'd moved into the flat above hers.

'It was bad enough when I rented the place to those university students,' she'd sniffed. 'Playing their stereos at all hours of the day and night, never shutting a door when they could bang it, but I refuse to have my eardrums blasted by a screaming child. No offence meant, Ms Hart, but I've always been a firm believer in speaking my mind.'

And speak it she had. Constantly.

But at least not today. For once Annie managed to tip-toe down the stairs and past Mrs Patterson's door without having to endure her usual catalogue of complaints. She'd undoubtedly have to hear them when she arrived home this afternoon, but at least she'd missed them this morning. Now all she had to do was to get Jamie to the centre, and herself to the hospital on time.

A task she had about as much hope of achieving as flying, she realised, glancing down at her watch with a groan.

'Where have you *been*?' Liz exclaimed when Annie flew into the staffroom at ten past eight. 'I've been stalling for you as long as I could but—'

'Is Woody blowing a fuse?' Annie interrupted, throwing her coat over one of the staffroom chairs.

'Luckily for you she's been on the telephone for the past fifteen minutes, trying to discover what's happened to the X-rays she ordered for Mrs Douglas. It's Gideon I've been stalling, and by now he must think you've got severe bladder problems.'

'Bladder problems?' Annie repeated, pausing in the middle of dragging on her white coat.

'I had to come up with *something* to explain your absence so I said you were in the loo. Now, for heaven's sake, get yourself along to his consulting room fast.'

Annie needed no second bidding. She was out the door, running. Head down, heart racing, along the corridor, round the corner, and to her utter horror slap bang into Gideon yet again.

'I'm sorry—so sorry,' she gasped, disentangling herself from his arms as fast as she could, red-cheeked with embarrassment.

'I'm not.' He grinned. 'In fact, I think I could get to quite like this. Not every day, of course—you can have too much of a good thing—but once in a while? Yup, I reckon I could live with that.'

He was joking—she knew he was—trying to make her feel better—but it didn't help.

Why did this have to keep on happening to her? She never used to be so inefficient. She never used to be so clumsy, and yet in less than a week at the Belfield she'd been late twice, trashed the contents of a tea trolley and now cannoned into her boss for the second time.

'I'm sorry,' she said unhappily. 'I know I'm late again.'

'I wondered about that. Liz kept telling me you were in the toilet, and I was beginning to think you might need to see me in a professional capacity.'

He was smiling but, try as she may she couldn't smile back. 'Please, don't blame Sister Baker—she was only trying to help. I had… There were problems at home.'

All amusement instantly disappeared from his face. 'Nothing serious, I hope?'

Just my son realising that when I leave him I'm going to be gone for hours. Just the question of what am I going to do tomorrow, or the day after, if the same thing happens again.

Tell him, her mind whispered, he'll understand.

But what if he didn't? The male doctors at the Manchester Infirmary had been anything but sympathetic when a female doctor was late, or distracted, because of family problems.

'Unreliable' had been one of their favourite comments. 'Not sufficiently committed' had been another. And always the implication had been the same. That it was a mistake to employ a female doctor with a young child.

'No, it was nothing serious,' she said. 'Everything's fine.'

'But—'

'Do I have time to look at the files of some of the patients you'll be seeing this morning?'

He knew she was changing the subject. He also looked as though he'd very much like to press her on why she'd been late, but abruptly he turned on his heel and led the way into his consulting room.

'Take your pick.'

She stared at his desk. Her pick? Good grief, there had to be at least fifty—if not more—files sitting there.

'How long did you say this clinic was supposed to last?' she asked involuntarily, only to colour when she suddenly realised how that might sound. 'Not that it matters, of course. I mean, that's what I'm here for—to learn, to assist. And I know we don't work nine to five, and—'

'Annie, I wasn't about to whip out a placard with the words "Poor attitude—lack of commitment" written on it,' he snapped. 'So relax, OK?'

The colour on her cheeks darkened. 'Yes. Sorry.'

'Half of those files belong to patients we'll be seeing today. The other half belong to patients I'll be seeing on Monday, and I'm taking them home with me for a quick read-through at the weekend.'

'Oh, right.' She nodded. 'Sorry.'

And I wish to heaven you'd stop apologising to me, Gideon thought, selecting the top file from the pile on his desk and handing it to her. The woman he'd met on the stairs might have got his intentions all wrong but at least she'd had some spunk about her. Lord, but she'd been angry that day, her blue eyes flashing, contempt plain on her face, but he'd liked her. He still did, but not when she behaved like some stressed-out, scared rabbit.

She'd said there'd been trouble at home. Could she be looking after an infirm or elderly relative—was that why she'd been late this morning? Her file might tell him but to get it he'd have to ask Admin, and he knew only too well what the gossiping girls who worked there would make of such a request.

'Mr Caldwell's interested in Annie Hart,' they'd snigger, and they'd be right.

But not in the silly, lovesick way they would mean. His interest was purely professional. Based solely on safeguarding the best interests of the department. And yet as he saw a small frown suddenly crease her forehead he couldn't help but wonder what it would take to make her smile—really smile. Dammit, she couldn't be any more than twenty-seven or twenty-eight, and yet she looked as though she carried all the cares of the world on her shoulders.

'Annie—'

'Miss Bannerman has fibroids?'

Well, it wasn't quite what he'd had in mind as a topic of conversation, but if talking about their first patient would make her relax he was more than willing to go with it.

'Carol was referred to me six months ago because of excessive menstrual pain and bleeding, and bladder problems.'

'The bladder problems would be due to the pressure of her fibroids?' she suggested, and he nodded.

'Fibroids—or benign tumours of the uterine muscle to give them their correct name—are very common amongst women over thirty-five. It's only when they start to interfere with a woman's life—as they have done in Carol's— that we need to do something about them.'

She handed him back the file. 'I notice you've been treating her with drugs.'

'Fibroids are caused by too much oestrogen in the body. If we can decrease the level, the fibroids usually shrink, and the pain and excessive bleeding lessens, but—'

'The drugs can't cure the fibroids, and as they tend to

have side-effects if taken for too long, it's not a long-term solution,' she finished for him.

He stared at her thoughtfully. Woody had said she was bright, and she obviously was, but bright doctors didn't necessarily make good ones. Annie could have all the book learning in the world, but if her communication skills with patients were as poor as they were with him…

He cleared his throat. 'On Carol's last visit I told her she really only had two options. A hysterectomy, or a laparoscopic myomectomy. She's coming in today to discuss those options, and I'd like you to advise her.'

'Me?' she faltered. 'But—'

'As you said yourself, you're here to learn.'

'Yes, but—'

'I'm not going to abandon you, Annie,' he said gently. 'I'll sit in—put in my pennyworth if you need it—but I think it would be a useful exercise, don't you?'

She obviously didn't, and he could see her point. Throwing her in at the deep end on her very first clinic was deeply unfair. It was also, as it turned out, a revelation.

The minute Carol Bannerman walked in, Annie became a different woman. Gone was the nervous, apologetic person he kept meeting, and in her place sat a calm, understanding professional. A professional who gently and simply outlined the two procedures, showing not a trace of impatience or irritation whenever Carol asked for clarification.

Which made her decision not to immediately apply for a junior doctor's position after she'd finished med school all the more puzzling. She was bright, confident—just so long as he wasn't around—so why had she put her career on hold for four years?

It was a mystery, and one he intended solving, but not right now. Not when it seemed that Carol had finally come to a decision.

'I want to have the laparoscopic myomectomy,' she declared. 'I know Mr Caldwell said my fibroids might come back if I had that, but to have a hysterectomy...' Tears filled Carol's eyes and she blinked them away quickly. 'I'm only thirty-six, Dr Hart, and my partner and I really want a baby.'

Annie glanced across at Gideon, but his face gave her no clue as to what he was thinking. Her brother always said that consultants who performed hysterectomies for fibroids were lazy surgeons, but if it was Gideon's preferred choice...

Go for it, Annie, she told herself. He asked you to advise Carol Bannerman, and if he doesn't like what you say, so be it.

'I see no reason why anyone should have a perfectly healthy uterus removed just to get rid of some benign tumours,' she said firmly.

'Then you agree with me?' Carol said uncertainly. 'You think I should have a myomectomy?'

Deliberately Annie avoided Gideon's gaze. 'Yes, I do. There's only one thing I should warn you about,' she continued when Carol let out a sigh of relief. 'If you do become pregnant after the myomectomy, you'll almost certainly need a Caesarean section to deliver. The procedure tends to weaken the uterine wall, you see.'

'A Caesarean sounds good to me,' Carol observed with a shaky laugh. 'Eliminate all that painful huff, puff and pant stuff, and just get the baby out.'

'If it was as simple as that, every mum-to-be would opt for one.' Annie smiled. 'But a Caesarean's not something to be undertaken lightly. It's an operation—a big one—and most women take six to eight weeks to recover from it. Not a very attractive proposition if you've a young baby to look after.'

'I'll cross that bridge when—if—I ever get to it,' Carol declared. 'How long will I have to stay in hospital?'

'I…um…' Annie glanced across at Gideon in mute appeal and he leant forward in his seat.

'A couple of days at most, and if everything goes to plan you should be back at work within a fortnight. It's not a difficult procedure,' he continued when Carol looked surprised.

But was it what he would have recommended? Annie wondered as he made a note in his appointment book. Surely it must be, or wouldn't he have contradicted her advice?

But he didn't say anything—not even after Carol had gone. To be fair, there wasn't really the time—not with a waiting room full of anxious, nervous women—but she thought he might have said *something*. Even if it had only been, 'Annie Hart, you're an idiot.'

'So what did you think of your first clinic?' was all he said when the last of their patients had finally gone.

'I enjoyed it,' she replied. 'Especially meeting your IVF patient—Mrs Norton. She was so thrilled to be pregnant.'

'I'm surprised she wasn't a little smug.'

'Smug?' she repeated in confusion.

'I wanted her to stop when her third IVF treatment failed. It's so emotionally devastating, you see, when the procedure doesn't work, but Jennifer was determined to give it one last try, and as it turns out she was right and I was wrong.'

He'd given her the opening she needed, and she took it. 'Carol Bannerman—the lady with fibroids. I was right, wasn't I, to suggest she opt for a myomectomy?'

His eyebrows rose. 'I think the more important question here is, do *you* think you were right?'

'But—'

'But me no buts, Annie. Do you think you advised the best possible course of treatment for her?'

Quickly she mentally reviewed Carol Bannerman's case notes, then took a deep breath. 'Yes. Yes, I do.'

For what seemed like an eternity he said nothing, then his lips curved. 'So do I.'

'Then why didn't you *say* so?' she protested, letting out the breath she hadn't even known she'd been holding. 'I've been sweating buckets all morning—'

'I noticed.'

'Why, you…you *rat*!' The words were out before she could stop them, and she flushed scarlet. 'I'm so sorry—'

'Please—oh, *please*, don't apologise,' he exclaimed, his face creasing into a broad smile. 'You're absolutely right. It *was* a rotten thing to do, but I was curious to see how long it would take you to crack and say something to me other than ''Sorry''.'

'Your entire clinic apparently,' she said ruefully, and his smile widened.

'That's better. That's what I've been wanting to see— some lightness about you, some humour.'

She bit her lip. 'I didn't realise I was so grim.'

His brown eyes caught and held hers. 'Not grim. Just tense, and nervous, and there's no need for you to be. I'm not an ogre, you know.'

No, he wasn't, she thought as she gazed up at him and felt her own lips curving in response to the smile on his. He was nice, and understanding, and…

This is a mistake, her mind warned. A big, big mistake. You're starting to like him. Not as your boss, but as a man, and remember what happened the last time you liked your boss—the heartache it caused, the devastation when he walked away. Do you want that again?

'Annie—'

'Good grief, is it a quarter to two already?' she exclaimed, catching sight of the clock on the wall behind him. 'I have to go.'

'But I was hoping we might have lunch together in the canteen,' he protested. 'I know you're supposed to go off duty today at one o'clock, but you can't call me a rat and then not give me the opportunity to prove to you that I'm actually a big soft teddy bear.'

Lunch with him in the canteen sounded appealing—far too appealing. Thank goodness she couldn't. Thank goodness she really did have to go.

'I'm sorry but I can't,' she said, quickly picking up her bag and heading for the door. 'I have to go shopping.'

'But, Annie—'

She'd gone, and he threw down his pen with frustration. What the hell had he said wrong *now*? For crying out loud, all he'd suggested was lunch in the canteen, and yet she'd shot out of his room as though he'd lit a fire under her. To go shopping.

He snorted derisively. He supposed it was marginally better than the old 'I'm washing my hair' routine, but why she'd needed to make up an excuse was beyond him. It wasn't as though he'd asked her for a date, just to join him for lunch in the canteen so they could get to know one another better. And he'd thought they were beginning to do just that when—

'Gideon, have you got any more of those cervical smear leaflets we give out to patients?' Helen asked, popping her head round his consulting-room door. 'There's none left in the waiting room.'

'If there's none left in the waiting room, get onto Admin,' he snapped. 'I'm not the local stationery office.'

'Right.' She nodded. 'Sorry.'

'Hell's bells, not you, too,' he groaned, then shook his head when his SHO's eyebrows rose. 'Sorry, Helen, but right now I've had my fill of people apologising to me.'

'Rough clinic?' she said sympathetically.

'Not the clinic. It's…' He struggled to find the right words, and gave up. 'Helen, do I seem like an ogre to you?'

'An ogre?' She stared at him in surprise. 'Of course you're not an ogre. Who said—?'

'Nobody,' he interrupted hurriedly. Lord, but he wished he'd never started this conversation. Especially not with Helen. 'It isn't important. Forget it.'

'Not on your life!' she exclaimed, her brown eyes sparkling. 'Come on—give. Who is she?'

'She?' he repeated faintly.

'Gideon, I've known you for almost seven years, and you've never terrified a patient in your life, so it's got to be a girl. Someone you desperately want to make a good impression on, or you wouldn't care two hoots whether she was terrified of you or not.'

He stared at her, open-mouthed, then shook his head. 'The processes of the female mind are wondrous to behold.'

'I'm right, though, aren't I?' Helen declared. 'Who is it? I hope it's not that busty new nurse in Paediatrics. She's not your type at all, and that frosty-faced receptionist in radiology would be a disaster.'

'Helen—'

'Which only leaves either the new nurse in A and E, or Annie Hart.'

To his dismay, hot colour began to creep across his cheeks. 'Helen—'

'It's Annie, isn't it?' she whooped with delight. 'Oh, Gideon, I'm so pleased. I know how much you loved Susan, but Annie's a sweet girl, and—'

'Helen, read my lips,' he said through gritted teeth. 'I am not—repeat not—interested in Dr Hart other than in a purely professional capacity.'

'You've had a row, right?' she commiserated. 'Look, it'll blow over. All you have to do is be your own sweet self, and she'll come round.'

And I'm surrounded by lunatics, Gideon thought dazedly as Helen's bleeper sounded and she hurried off to answer it. All I asked was whether I was an ogre and immediately my SHO's hearing wedding bells. With

Annie Hart, of all people. OK, so she's a very pretty girl, and she clearly needs somebody to take care of her, but it isn't going to be me. No way. Not ever.

But it felt good when you were holding her, didn't it? his mind whispered. Every time she's tumbled into your arms it's felt right, almost as though she somehow—oddly—belonged there. And what about the feel of her slender waist beneath your fingers, the soft curve of her breasts—so high and surprisingly full—and—

He swore under his breath as his body suddenly reacted with unbridled enthusiasm to the picture his mind had just created. How long had it been since he'd been out with a woman—two, maybe three years? It had obviously been far too long, but he'd been so busy since Susan had died with all the interminable meetings that were part and parcel of his job. The clinics, the operations, the ward rounds...

Excuses, Gideon, his mind whispered as he strode out of his room, and not very good ones at that. You haven't dated anyone since Susan died because you're scared to get close to anyone again in case you lose them, too. It's fear that's kept you celibate, not work.

'Oh, shut up,' he muttered just as Tom Brooke came out of his room. 'No, not you, Tom,' he continued when the specialist registrar looked startled. 'I'm just having a bad day, that's all.'

'Join the club,' Tom sighed. 'Are you coming down to the canteen for lunch?'

Gideon shook his head. 'I think I might just do a quick ward round, then get off home.'

'Good idea.' Tom nodded. 'You look as though you could do with some rest.'

He sure as heck needed something, Gideon decided after he'd toured the ward then made his way down to the car park. And it wasn't Helen sticking her oar in. OK, so his long-dormant hormones seemed to have unexpectedly kicked into life, but that didn't mean he had to act on them. It didn't mean he was *interested*—in the sense of being interested—in Annie Hart.

He had a lot more important things to think about anyway, he told himself as he drove down Rottenrow, then along Richmond Road and into Duke Street. Like getting home, for a start. He should have left the hospital earlier, of course. The traffic was always murder on a Friday afternoon, and today it was even slower because of the icy roads and driving sleet.

At least he was warm and cosy in his car, he thought as he drummed his fingers absently on the steering-wheel, waiting for the van ahead of him to move. Not like the poor people out on the street. People like…

Annie. He'd have recognised her anywhere, and she hadn't been lying about the shopping. She was lugging four obviously very heavy carrier bags up the road, and she looked wet, and cold, and miserable.

Without a second's thought he cut in towards the pavement, ignoring the cacophony of car horns that greeted his manoeuvre, and parked beside her.

'M-Mr Caldwell,' she stammered as he got out of his car. 'Is there something wrong—at the hospital—?'

'The name's Gideon, and nothing's wrong at the hospital, but you look in serious need of a lift home.'

She shook her head. 'It's kind of you to offer, but I just live round the corner in Thornton Street.'

Which was a good half a mile away if he remembered rightly, and all of it uphill. He opened his passenger door. 'Get in, Annie.'

'No, honestly, there's no need—'

'Annie, I'm illegally parked on double yellow lines, so unless you want me to get a ticket from that traffic warden who's bearing down on us, please, get in the car.'

She did so with obvious reluctance, and when they arrived in Thornton Street she even more reluctantly allowed him to carry her groceries up to her top-floor flat.

He wasn't surprised. Given how edgy she always was in his company, he'd have been amazed if she'd welcomed his offer of help, but what did surprise him—horrified him, if he was honest—was her flat.

'It has a lovely view of the cathedral,' she said defensively, clearly sensing his dismay as he carried her groceries through to the tiny kitchen. 'And it's near to the hospital.'

Yes, but it's the most depressing place I've ever seen, he wanted to reply. OK, so it was clean and tidy, and the few pieces of furniture gleamed with much polishing, but its dark green wallpaper would have given him nightmares, and as for the chipped and peeling paintwork…

'How long have you lived here?' he asked.

'Two months.'

Two minutes would have been more than enough for him. 'Annie—'

'Would you like a cup of coffee before you go?'

Subtle she wasn't, but he had no intention of leaving. Not yet, at any rate. Junior doctor's salaries weren't exactly lavish, but surely a single woman could have afforded something better than this?

'I'll help you unpack first,' he said firmly. 'And, yes, I know you don't need any help,' he continued when she opened her mouth, patently intending to protest, 'but just humour me, please, hmm?'

Gideon didn't wait for her reply. Instead, he determinedly began emptying her grocery bags, but the more packets and tins he placed on the kitchen table, the more confused he became. Spaghetti hoops, Twinkie bars, lollipops. What kind of weird diet was she on?

'Far be it for me to criticise,' he observed, reaching down into one of the bags to retrieve what looked like

Beanie biscuits, 'but if this is a sample of your eating habits, I think you badly need some nutritional advice.'

She opened her mouth, closed it again, then seemed to come to a decision. 'They're not for me. They're…they're for my son.'

His hand stilled. 'I didn't realise you were married.'

'I'm not. And I'm not divorced either,' she continued as his eyebrows rose. 'I'm a single parent.'

He stared at her silently. It explained so much. Answered so many questions, and yet raised a whole lot more.

'Your son—he's four, isn't he?'

'Yes, but how—?'

'It didn't require much genius to figure it out,' he declared as she stared at him in astonishment. 'You took four years out between finishing med school and applying for the post at the Belfield, so…' He shrugged. 'Was that why you were late this morning—because of your son?'

'It won't happen again,' she said quickly. 'He didn't want to go to the day-care centre, you see, but I promise it won't happen again.'

'Hell's bells, Annie, your son is your first priority, not the bloody hospital,' he snapped, then bit his lip when she flinched. 'I'm sorry, I didn't mean to yell, but I do understand. I know the kind of pressure Helen faces with her two kids—'

'I don't want—or need—any allowances made for me.'

But she did, he thought. Every working mother needed help sometimes. 'Annie—'

He came to a halt as her front doorbell rang, and when she went to answer it he stayed in the kitchen. He would have remained there, too, if the increasingly strident sound of a female voice hadn't aroused his curiosity.

'Is there something wrong?' he asked, emerging from the kitchen in time to see a dumpy, middle-aged woman brandishing a toy truck under Annie's nose.

'It's nothing,' Annie said quickly. 'Please, go back in the kitchen.'

Not on your life, he thought, seeing the woman glance from him to Annie with a look he didn't care for.

'I'm Gideon Caldwell—a friend of Annie's,' he said, holding out his hand. 'And you are…?'

The woman didn't unbend an inch. In fact, she bristled even more.

'Mrs Patterson, the landlady, and as I've just been telling Ms Hart, this is the fourth time I've found this toy lying outside my door.'

'And you brought it back for her—how very kind of you,' he said smoothly.

'Kindness had nothing to do it,' she snapped. 'It shouldn't have been there in the first place.'

'I'll speak to Jamie,' Annie said hurriedly. 'Make sure it doesn't happen again.'

'You keep saying that, and it's not good enough,' Mrs Patterson retorted. 'He's always leaving his toys lying about, and he was running up and down again this morning. Thump, thump, thump, from seven o'clock onwards. I could rent this flat to anyone, Ms Hart—'

'Did you advertise this flat as being unsuitable for children?' Gideon interrupted.

Mrs Patterson stared at him. 'I beg your pardon?'

'When you advertised this flat, did you specifically stipulate it was unsuitable for young children?' he asked, his voice hard, cold.

'No, but—'

'Then so long as Dr Hart pays her rent, I think you should take yourself, and your veiled threats, elsewhere, don't you?'

Mrs Patterson's mouth fell open. She turned a quite amazing shade of red, then with a fulminating look at Annie she banged out the door, leaving Annie gazing after her.

'Well, I think I sorted that out, don't you?' Gideon smiled, but to his surprise Annie didn't look pleased. She looked furious.

'Sorted it out?' she repeated. 'All you've done is made things ten times worse!'

'But—'

'She's already on my back twice a day.'

'Then move out—get somewhere else.'

Her colour changed from fiery red to white, then back to red again. 'Do you have *any* idea how difficult it is for a woman with a young child to get affordable rented accommodation in Glasgow?'

'No, but—'

'It took me almost six months to find this place—'

'You should have kept looking.'

She clenched her hands together until her knuckles showed white. 'OK, that does it. You waltz in here uninvited, sneer at my home—oh, yes, you did,' she continued as he tried to protest, 'and then you antagonise my landlady. I think you've more than outstayed your welcome, don't you?'

'Annie—'

'Goodbye, Mr Caldwell.'

'The name's Gideon,' he said in exasperation. 'G-I-D-E-O-N. Good grief, it's not that hard to pronounce.'

'And the door is right behind you,' she said pointedly.

He wondered if he should remind her that he hadn't had his coffee yet, but one look at her furious face told him it would be a mistake. She'd undoubtedly give it to him all right. Right over his head.

Well, fine, he thought as he strode out the door. If she didn't want his help, then fine. If she wanted to be intimidated by a harridan landlady, and live with her son in a depressing flat, then that was fine, too. He washed his hands of her.

He had better things to do than worry about a girl with

corn-coloured curls and large blue eyes who probably had to lug heavy shopping bags up that steep hill every week. Much better things. And if he couldn't think of a single thing at the moment, he sure as heck soon would.

CHAPTER THREE

SYLVIA RENTON stirred uncomfortably in her bed and sighed as Annie took her blood pressure.

'You know, doctor, the ironic thing is I always wanted a baby. Even when I was a child, I pictured myself married with a baby of my own, but I never thought it would be like this. I expected to have a little morning sickness—all pregnant women do—but I never thought I'd still be throwing up at seven months.'

'Most women aren't,' Annie said sympathetically. 'Morning sickness—or Hyperemesis gravidarum to give it its proper medical name—normally stops after twelve to fourteen weeks.'

'Then why hasn't it stopped for me?' the patient protested. 'I've been doing all the right things—eating dry crackers, making sure my meals were small and regular—but still nothing stays down.'

And it showed, Annie thought as she sat down on the edge of Sylvia's bed. Not only was the woman's weight gain far too low for a seven-month pregnancy, she was in real danger of becoming dehydrated, which was why Gideon had hospitalised her.

'I'm afraid I don't know why you've been affected like this,' Annie said. 'Some experts think it's because the placenta is producing very high levels of a hormone called chorionic gonadotrophin. Others believe the baby itself could be raising your oestrogen levels. The only thing we know for certain is that it tends to be more common in women carrying twins or triplets.'

'Mr Caldwell's done all the tests, and I'm only carrying one.'

'I know.' Annie nodded. 'Which seems to suggest you're just one of nature's unlucky ones.'

Tears welled in Sylvia's eyes. 'I don't want to be one of nature's unlucky ones. I want you to *do* something— give me something—to make me feel better. I'm only twenty-four, but I feel a hundred and four.'

'Sylvia—'

'My husband said that if you give me drugs it might be harmful to the baby, but do you know something, Dr Hart? Right now I don't give a damn about side-effects. Right now I don't give a damn about anything—including this baby. All I want is for you to stop me feeling so awful all the time.'

It was an understandable request, Annie thought as she walked slowly back down the ward. OK, so the actuality of being pregnant rarely mirrored the glossy pictures in the mums-and-babies magazines, but to be constantly sick for seven months, then hospitalised, and having to exist solely on electrolyte replacement and enriched fluids through an IV line couldn't be much fun.

'Any word of when I'm going to get something to eat, Doctor?' Kay Wilson shouted from her bed by the window. 'Giving birth is hard work, you know.'

Annie smiled back. 'Sorry, but it's nil by mouth for you for the rest of the day. We want to find out if the high levels of sugar which appeared in your urine when you were pregnant have disappeared now you've given birth, or whether they're still there.'

'You mean I'm not even going to get a cup of tea?' Kay protested. 'Doctor, I'll fade away.'

It was highly unlikely, Annie thought with a wry, inward chuckle. By any definition Kay was a seriously big girl.

'Hey, look on the bright side,' she said encouragingly. 'Think how wonderful food is going to taste when you finally get it.'

'I'd far rather taste it now than think about it,' Kay complained, and Annie laughed, but her laughter died as she glanced back down the ward at Sylvia.

She hadn't heard the girl laugh once since she'd been admitted, but what was even more worrying was that she was clearly starting to resent her baby. If the resentment continued after the child was born...

'Problems?' Helen asked, seeing her lost in thought.

'It's Mrs Renton,' Annie replied. 'She's feeling really wretched, and I can't say I blame her. Seven months of morning sickness would depress anyone.'

'The trouble is, we've got to balance the benefits of giving her drugs to stop the sickness against the possible damaging side-effects to the baby,' Helen replied. 'The last thing we want is a repetition of the thalidomide disaster.'

Annie nodded. There wasn't a doctor in the UK who didn't know about that particular catastrophe, when pregnant women had given birth to babies with stunted and deformed limbs after they'd been treated for hyperemesis gravidarum.

'Something wrong?' Gideon asked, glancing from Helen's pensive face to Annie's worried one as he joined them.

'It's Sylvia Renton,' Helen replied. 'Annie thinks she's getting very low psychologically.'

Gideon bit his lip and frowned. 'I've been half expecting this, but... How often does her husband visit?'

'Every day,' Annie answered, 'but she scarcely says more than two words to him.'

Gideon's frown deepened. 'How do you get on with her?'

'Me? OK, I guess,' she said uncertainly. 'I mean, we talk a bit, and I think she likes me—'

'Good. Keep on talking to her. Give her as much emotional support as you can. It looks as though I'll have to perform a Caesarean eventually but I'd like to wait as long as possible to give the baby the best chance of survival.'

'Do you want me to report to you if I think there's any further deterioration in her mental condition?' she asked, and Gideon shook his head.

'If you tell either Helen or Tom, that will be fine.'

Well, what had she expected? Annie thought as he walked away. Considering she'd all but thrown him out of her flat last week, she could hardly expect him to want to spend any time in her company now.

Which was just fine. After all, it wasn't as though she *wanted* to spend time with him. A simple boss and junior doctor relationship suited her just perfectly. It did. And if she found herself missing the smiles he'd greeted her with before, well, that was just plain stupid.

'Gideon's a very decent bloke, you know.'

Helen was gazing at her thoughtfully, and Annie said nothing. She thought plenty. She thought of telling the SHO that decent blokes didn't waltz into people's houses uninvited. Decent blokes didn't interfere where they had no business to interfere. But she said nothing.

'He met his wife at the Belfield,' Helen continued, as she led the way into the staffroom and switched on the kettle. 'Susan was an SHO in Paediatrics, and he was a specialist registrar in Obs and Gynae. He was absolutely devastated when she died. In fact, there was a time when Tom and I really thought he might not make it through.'

'Did you?' Annie murmured noncommittally, wondering why on earth the SHO was telling her all this.

'He desperately needs someone in his life again,' Helen commented, spooning some coffee into two mugs, 'but the trouble is, he's got right out of the habit of talking to women. Oh, he's great with our female patients, but in a personal situation...' She shook her head. 'He puts himself down too much, and I don't think he realises how attractive he is.'

And I still don't know why you're telling me this, Annie thought, accepting the mug Helen was holding out to her. It's none of my business. If Gideon can't string more than two words together when he's alone with a woman, it would still be none of my business.

Neither was he attractive. OK, so he had a nice face and a nice smile, but he wasn't attractive. Nick had been attractive. Actually, Nick had been totally gorgeous. And fickle, and disloyal, and a louse.

'Annie, the very girl I'm looking for.' Liz beamed, bouncing into the staffroom. 'I just happen to have a few tickets left for the St Valentine's Ball a week on Friday—'

'A few?' Annie exclaimed, her eyes widening at the bundle Liz had produced from her pocket. 'Good grief, it's not exactly the hottest date in town, is it?'

Liz grimaced. 'OK, so you've rumbled me. These tickets are proving harder to shift than Mrs Gill's constipation, and I can't understand it. When we first suggested throwing a ball for Valentine's Day everybody was all for it, but now…'

'I'll buy two tickets from you,' Helen said, extracting her purse from her handbag. 'Tom and I haven't been to a dance for ages.'

A slight flush of colour appeared on Liz's plump cheeks. 'I…I understood from your husband that you and he had plans for that night, Dr Fraser.'

Helen looked puzzled, then her eyes lit up. 'He's taking me out, isn't he? I gave him hell last year because he forgot to send me a card, and this year he's taking me out as a surprise. Are we going to Stephano's? Oh, come on, Liz,' she pressed as the girl looked even more uncomfortable. 'If it's somewhere really posh I want to buy a new dress and get my hair done.'

'It's…well, he's not actually taking you out, Dr Fraser,' Liz mumbled. 'There's a big European football match being televised that night, and he said he was really looking forward to it.'

All excitement and enthusiasm disappeared from Helen's face in an instant, and her voice when she spoke was tight. 'So I'm going to be stuck in my own sitting room on St Valentine's Day while he watches a football match, am I? Right. We'll just see about that.'

'Dr Fraser—'

She was gone before Liz could stop her, and the girl slumped into one of the staffroom chairs with a groan. 'Brilliant, Liz—just brilliant. Now Tom isn't going to be speaking to me until Christmas.'

'It's not your fault,' Annie said gently. 'Look, do you want a coffee? Dr Fraser didn't drink hers.'

'I'd far rather sell you a couple of these damned tickets. Oh, come on, Annie,' Liz begged when she shook her head. 'We've hired the function room in the Grosvenor Hotel and at this rate the St Valentine's Ball is going to consist of ten couples, the band and me.'

'I really can't—I'm sorry.'

'Hot date for that night, I suppose?' Liz said gloomily.

For a second Annie hesitated, but as Gideon already knew she had a child it seemed silly not to say anything.

'A very hot date,' she said nodding, 'and he's blond, blue-eyed and two feet four. It's my son.' She chuckled when Liz gazed at her blankly. 'And as I get to see so little of him nowadays, what with me working all day, I like to spend all my free time with him.'

'Then bring him along to the ball. OK—all right—so it's a dumb idea,' Liz declared when Annie laughed, 'but I'm getting desperate. There's got to be somebody I can sell these damn tick—' She sprang to her feet as Rachel Dunwoody passed the staffroom door. 'Doctor, could I interest you in a ticket for the St Valentine's Ball?'

Rachel shook her head. 'I don't think so, thank you.'

'But it'll be great fun,' Liz persisted. 'Lots of people are going—'

'Lots of young couples, you mean. Thanks, Liz, but it's not really my sort of thing.'

'I'm going on my own,' Liz exclaimed. 'And you're not old, Doctor. Good grief you can't be any more than thirty-five.'

'I'm twenty-nine, actually,' Rachel Dunwoody said stiffly.

'And why don't I just shoot myself—save everybody else the bother?' Liz wailed as Woody stalked away. 'How the hell was I supposed to know she was only twenty-nine? With that hairdo, and her manner...'

'Have a biscuit,' Annie offered, opening the tin. 'Better yet—take two.'

Liz did. 'This ball is going to be a total fiasco.'

'No, it won't,' Annie said encouragingly. 'In fact, I bet the nearer you get to next Friday the faster those tickets will fly out of your hand.'

Liz didn't look convinced. 'I don't know why we bother with St Valentine's Day in the first place,' she said belligerently. 'It only causes a lot of heartache if you don't get a card.'

Tell me about it, Annie thought, remembering the Valentine's Day before Jamie was born. She'd been so much in love with Nick, and he hadn't even sent her a card. Oh, he'd dashed out the next day and bought her a dozen red roses, but it hadn't been the same.

'Frankly, I'd far rather somebody gave me an occasional bunch of pansies or freesias to show they were thinking of me instead of a card once a year,' Annie said, trying and failing to keep the edge out of her voice. 'And now I'd better get back to the ward or I'll be having my head in my hands.'

Probably considerably more than her head, she thought

with a groan when she walked out of the staffroom to find Gideon standing in the corridor.

How long had he been there? Hopefully not long. She was entitled to a coffee-break—of course she was—but he might think she'd have been better employed using it to read medical textbooks rather than chatting about St Valentine's Day.

'Were you looking for me?' she asked uncertainly.

He nodded. 'I want you to have a word with the patient in room 3. She was brought into A and E this morning with suspected appendicitis, but I've examined her and I'm pretty certain she's actually suffering from pelvic inflammatory disease. The problem is, she wants to discharge herself and is point-blank refusing to allow me to schedule her for an exploratory laparoscopy. I'm hoping you might be able to persuade her otherwise.'

'M-me?' she stammered. 'But—'

'She's only eighteen, Annie, and I thought if you talked to her privately—woman to woman… Look, give it your best shot, will you?' he continued, seeing the misgivings in her face. 'I'll wait outside, come in if you get into difficulties, but I really—*really*—don't want her to leave.'

Neither did Annie, but she honestly didn't see how she could succeed where Gideon had failed. Especially when she saw Louise Harper's tear-stained but defiant face.

'I'm Annie Hart, Louise,' she said in what she hoped was her most encouraging voice. 'Mr Caldwell asked me to have a word with you, and—'

'And I want to go home,' the girl interrupted. 'I know my rights. You can't keep me here—'

'No, we can't,' Annie interrupted gently, 'but I think it might be sensible if you stayed at least for the night with us, don't you? You're obviously in a lot of pain—'

'It'll go away. I've had it before, and it always goes away as soon as my periods have finished.'

'But what if it doesn't go away—what if it's even more painful next time?' Annie asked. The girl turned her face to the wall, and Annie pulled a chair forward and sat down beside her bed. 'Louise, listen to me. I know you're frightened and upset, but if you do have pelvic inflammatory disease, it isn't going to disappear simply because you refuse to think about it.'

'I can't have a sexually transmitted disease—I simply can't,' the girl sobbed into her pillow. 'I don't sleep around, Doctor. In fact, I've only ever made love with two men, and one of those is my current boyfriend. What's he going to say if he finds out I've got a sexually transmitted disease?'

Many a man had dumped his girlfriend for less, but now wasn't the time to tell Louise that. Not when her health was at stake.

'Louise, not all PID is caused by a sexually transmitted disease. Some of it is caused by bacteria normally found in your vagina and cervix which for some unknown reason has decided to migrate into your uterus.'

'But most of it is caused by gonorrhoea, and chlamydia, isn't it?'

Yes, was the honest answer, but Annie didn't say it.

'I think the most important thing is to find out if you've actually *got* the infection, don't you?' she said instead. 'And the only way we can do that is to perform a laparoscopy. We have to find out, Louise,' she continued as another sob came from the bed. 'If pelvic inflammatory disease isn't treated, it can irreparably damage your Fallopian tubes and your ovaries so when you want to have a baby, you can't.'

For a moment there was complete silence from the bed, then Louise turned her tear-stained face towards her. 'Would my boyfriend have to know?'

'I think you should tell him, don't you?'

'He'll dump me.'

'Not if he truly loves you, he won't. Look, will you at least stay overnight with us?' Annie pressed. 'Think seriously about having the laparoscopy? I'm sure Mr Caldwell could fit you in really quickly.'

At least she thought he could. She was pretty sure he could.

'It's not a big operation, Louise,' she continued when the girl said nothing. 'The scar on your tummy will be tiny—no more than an inch across—and surely it's better to know what's wrong with you rather than simply hoping it will go away.'

'But what if it is PID?' the girl exclaimed.

'Then we can treat it,' Annie said firmly. 'And the quicker we start treating it with antibiotics, the more likely we are to cure it.'

'I…I guess so,' Louise said hesitantly.

'Then you'll stay in hospital?'

Louise bit her lip. 'OK.'

Should she push it that little bit more, or settle for what she'd got? Push it, Annie, a little voice whispered, push it.

'And can I tell Mr Caldwell to schedule your laparoscopy for as soon as possible?'

For a second she wondered if she ought to have settled for what she'd got, then Louise said in a small voice, 'All right.'

It was a lot better than all right, Annie thought with relief as she left the room, and Gideon clearly agreed with her.

'Well done.' He beamed. 'Very, *very* well done.'

'I'm just so relieved,' she admitted. 'I wondered if perhaps I was pushing my luck, trying to get her to agree to the laparoscopy.'

'I wondered about that, too.' He nodded, leading the way into his consulting room. 'But you did it, and I'm very grateful.'

'I didn't tell her that one in five women who have PID become sterile,' she said uncertainly. 'I know I should have…'

'Sufficient unto the day, Annie. We'll tell her about the possibility of sterility after she's had the exploratory op. There's no point in adding more worries to that young lady's shoulders.'

'Will you be able to do the laparoscopy quickly?' she asked. 'I sort of promised, you see.'

'I heard.' He grinned. 'And it's no problem.' He consulted his operating book. 'I'm fully booked in Theatre tomorrow, but Friday—I could squeeze her in on Friday. Would you like to assist me? In fact, why don't you spend the whole morning with me in the operating theatre? It's high time you got some surgical experience.'

'You mean it?' she exclaimed with delight, and he nodded.

'It seems only fair, considering at least one of the patients we'll be operating on wouldn't be there if it weren't for you.' He made a note in his book, then glanced up at her. 'You're very good with people. No, you are, Annie,' he continued, seeing her shake her head. 'A lot of doctors have the knowledge, the expertise, but that's not the same as actually caring about people. The caring doctors are the ones patients remember after they've been discharged, and you're one of them.'

So was he, she thought, and yet she'd been so rude to him last week. Rude and awful when he'd probably only been trying to help. All right, so she hadn't wanted his help, but…

'I owe you an apology, don't I?' she said quickly, before she got cold feet. 'Last week—when I threw you out of my flat—'

'Annie—'

'No, please, let me finish,' she insisted. 'I know it's not a very great flat, and the landlady is a nightmare, but it took me so long to find it, and... Well, despite all its problems, it's the first real home I've had for me and Jamie.'

'And I stormed in with all the subtlety of a ten-ton truck,' he sighed. 'Is your landlady giving you a lot of grief over what I said?'

'No more than usual,' she lied, not wanting him to feel bad, but he knew she was lying and felt worse.

'Annie, I'm sorry—truly sorry. I know I shouldn't have interfered, but the trouble is I'm so used to organising things—people, the department, the ward—and if I see something unfair I tend to go in with both guns blazing.'

'I noticed.' She smiled, and his lips curved ruefully.

'Does that mean I'm forgiven? Please, say it does, because I'd very much like us to be friends. Not because I want to interfere in your life,' he continued quickly, seeing her blue eyes grow wary. 'I promise I won't do that, but just to be there if you ever need help. To be there if you need a friend.'

She'd like that, too, she realised, and being friends with him wasn't the same as becoming emotionally involved. Being friends was something she could handle.

'Friends, Gideon,' she agreed, holding out her hand to him, and his face lit up.

'You remembered my first name at last!'

She laughed, too, but when his hand enveloped hers all desire to laugh deserted her.

If they were simply friends, why was her heart quickening the way it was? If they were just friends, why was she suddenly so aware of him?

And she was aware. Not simply aware that this was a man she could grow to like, but aware of *him*. His maleness, the warm pressure of his fingers around hers, and the fact that Helen had been right. He *was* an attractive man.

OK, so he wasn't handsome in the way Nick had been

handsome, and he didn't possess half of Nick's winning charm, but there was something about him.

Perhaps it was his big broad shoulders which suggested safety, security. Perhaps it was the gentle smile on his lips which said, Trust me, I'll look after you. Or perhaps—if she was honest with herself—it was because he seemed to have reawakened feelings and needs in her she'd thought—hoped—were long since dead. Whatever it was, it was a potent combination, and every self-preserving instinct she possessed shrieked, *Run*.

'I…I must go,' she said, quickly extracting her hand from his, horribly aware that her cheeks must be red. 'It's after four, you see, and Jamie—'

'Annie—'

She'd shot out the door before he could stop her, and he threw his eyes heavenwards with exasperation.

He'd done it again. He didn't know how—or what he'd said—but he'd done it again.

One minute they'd been shaking hands, and she'd been smiling at him—such a lovely smile it had been, too— and the next she'd bolted.

She's neurotic, his mind whispered, and he shook his head firmly. Not neurotic, but edgy and nervous, and if he ever got his hands on the man who'd made her like that, he'd…

Sign himself immediately into a psychiatric ward before he totally lost the plot, he thought ruefully. And he *was* losing it.

Good grief, she was only a very new, very junior member of his department, and yet since she'd arrived at the Belfield he seemed to have spent nine-tenths of his time thinking about her.

Well, of course he did, Gideon told himself. She obviously needed somebody to watch out for her, and what better man than him to do it? Someone who had absolutely no intention of becoming emotionally involved with her. Someone who wouldn't hurt her as she'd obviously been very badly hurt in the past.

Perhaps he could buy her something to prove not all men were rats with ulterior motives? Something innocuous and unthreatening that a friend would give. Something like… Flowers. He'd heard her telling Liz how much she liked freesias and pansies, so maybe he could buy her something like that?

'Gideon, I need you to check through these statistical sheets with me.'

'Not now, Woody,' he said, clipping his bleeper to his belt. 'I have to go out.'

Rachel Dunwoody looked at him blankly. 'Out? But—'

'I'll be forty-five minutes, tops, but right now I have to go out.'

The florist was busy, but not busy enough, he discovered when one of the salesgirls bore down on him determinedly.

'Can I help you at all, sir?' she said, just as he picked up a spray of carnations.

He put the flowers down again quickly. 'I…um…I'm just looking, thank you.'

'We've some lovely red roses, sir,' the girl persisted. 'Roses are always very acceptable to that special lady in your life.'

'She's not special—well, she is, but…' Oh, lord, but this had been a very bad idea. The last time he'd bought flowers had been for Susan, and to start buying them now… Awkwardly he began backing towards the shop door, but the assistant was made of sterner stuff.

'Is it for her birthday, sir?' she pressed. 'An anniversary—the arrival of a new baby?'

'It's a gift,' he replied, desperately trying to fight down the tide of colour he could feel creeping across his cheeks. 'I was looking for a gift—for a friend.'

'Lilies, then, sir?' she suggested, picking up some enormous blooms. 'Lilies are always very popular.'

'Haven't you got anything smaller? I was thinking more on the lines of some pansies, or maybe freesias.'

'Pansies?' the girl repeated, clearly marking him down as the biggest cheapskate of all time. 'I don't think…' She paused and to Gideon's utter mortification shouted across the shop, 'Sandy, the gentleman's looking for pansies—have we got any?'

'Look, it doesn't matter,' he said, cringing inwardly as every eye in the shop turned towards him. 'I'll buy her chocolates instead—'

'You're in luck, sir,' Sandy declared, bustling towards them. 'We've got a couple of bunches in stock. How would you like them? In a bouquet—a posy—an arrangement?' she continued as he gazed at her blankly. 'To be delivered, or taken with you?'

'In a sort of posy-type thing,' he muttered. 'And I'll take them with me.'

And never ever set foot in this shop again, he thought grimly as the girl began wrapping the flowers in some colourful paper.

'I didn't expect to see you this evening, David,' Annie exclaimed as she ushered her brother through to her sitting room.

'I thought I'd just stop by, see how you were doing,' he replied, reaching out to catch Jamie as his nephew hurtled towards him with a shriek of delight. 'And find out how you're getting on with your ordinary—but not that ordinary—boss.'

'Fine, thank you,' she said evenly.

'That sounds promising.'

'David, he's my boss, end of story,' Annie insisted, annoyingly aware that the warmth she could feel edging across her cheeks was totally belying her words.

'A boss who rushes in like a knight in shining armour to thwart your grumpy landlady? Sounds more like the beginning of a nice romance to me.'

'David.'

'OK, OK—if you don't want to tell me, then don't,' he declared, ruffling Jamie's blond hair affectionately. 'I'll find out eventually.'

He would, too, Annie thought ruefully. He always did.

'Would you like a cup of coffee?' she asked, deliberately changing the subject, only to groan when she heard her front doorbell.

Surely it couldn't be Mrs Patterson again? She'd already endured one long diatribe from her landlady this afternoon, and the last thing she needed was another one.

But it wasn't Mrs Patterson on her doorstep. It was Gideon, looking uncharacteristically ill at ease and uncomfortable.

'I can't stay long,' he said quickly. 'I just wondered if I might have a word?'

'Of course you can,' she replied, ushering him down the hall, but when they reached the sitting room Gideon came to an uncertain halt.

'I didn't realise you had company.'

'I haven't—it's just David.' She smiled. 'David, this is my boss—Gideon Caldwell. Gideon, this is—'

'Jamie,' Gideon finished for her.

His voice sounded odd. Thick and slightly constricted. His eyes were riveted on Jamie with an expression Annie didn't understand. She glanced across at David questioningly but he was no help at all. In fact, from the grin on his face, he seemed to be finding something strangely amusing.

Well, somebody had to say something, she decided, so she said the first thing that came into her head. 'What lovely flowers.'

Gideon stared down at the posy in his hand, almost, she thought, as though he'd forgotten they were there.

'They're a gift,' he muttered. 'For…for one of my patients.'

'Oh, how very kind,' she exclaimed. 'Which one?'

'I mean…I meant an ex-patient,' he said quickly. 'Someone…someone before your time.'

'Do I scent the hint of a romance here, Mr Caldwell?' David asked, his blue eyes dancing.

'Certainly not,' Gideon exclaimed, his cheeks reddening. 'She— The patient and I—'

'Would you like a cup of coffee, Gideon?' Annie interrupted, shooting a glance at her brother which said, Stop it.

'No—thank you. I'd better get back to the hospital.'

He was halfway down the hall before Annie caught up with him.

'But I thought you said you wanted a word with me?' she protested.

'It'll keep. It wasn't that important anyway.'

Important enough for you to leave the hospital, she wanted to say. Important enough for you to drive all the way over here. But before she could say anything he'd gone, and she shook her head as she went back to the sitting room.

'David, that was seriously weird. One minute he's standing there, saying he wants a word with me, and the next…'

'I'm not surprised he left.'

'You're not?' she said in confusion.

'Those flowers. He brought them for you.'

'Rubbish,' she protested. 'You heard what he said.'

'Yeah, I heard.'

'David, if he'd brought me flowers, he'd have given them to me,' she said with exasperation.

'Not if he figured we were lovers—that I was Jamie's father.'

Her jaw dropped. 'Why in the world would he think that?'

Her brother smiled at her affectionately. 'You know, for a pretty smart lady, you can be awfully dumb at times. Look at this,' he continued, tugging at his hair as she scowled at him. 'It's blond, like Jamie's blond, and my eyes are blue—'

'So are mine.'

'And I'm sitting here in your flat, like I belong. The poor guy's put two and two together and come up with twenty-five.'

It made sense, and she supposed she ought to have found it funny, but she didn't. She half started towards the door, then stopped.

'Go after him, love,' her brother said, watching her. 'Explain who I am.'

It was what she wanted to do, what a very large part of her wanted to do, but…

'It's better this way,' she murmured.

'Better—or safer?' David shook his head. 'Annie, using me as a smokescreen so you don't have to face up to reality, admit you might actually have feelings—needs— that someone like Gideon Caldwell could answer, is the coward's way out.'

She didn't answer him—couldn't. Didn't even want to consider that her brother might possibly be right.

Instead, she scooped Jamie off his knee and said, 'I think it's time for your bath, young man.'

CHAPTER FOUR

'YOU'RE looking distinctly harassed this morning, Annie,' Tom declared as they scrubbed up together at the sinks. 'Anything I can help you with?'

Only if you know a cast-iron way of persuading my brother to keep his interfering nose out of my business. Only if you can dream up something that will make my son go willingly to the day-care centre again without having to be constantly bribed. And only if you can put an end to the dreams I keep having about Gideon Caldwell. Dreams which are silly and stupid, and make me feel hot and embarrassed whenever I remember them.

'I'm just suffering from a bad attack of February blues, that's all,' she replied lightly.

'Gideon's been a bit down, too, these last couple of days,' Tom observed, turning off the tap with his elbow. 'Kind of grouchy, wouldn't you say?'

She would, but she preferred not to think about it.

'Carol Bannerman's our first patient this morning, isn't she?' she said instead.

Tom nodded. 'Gideon should be doing her op, but he's in Theatre 2 because of that multiple pile-up on the M8. One of the drivers is eight months pregnant and it looks touch and go for both her and her baby.'

Annie had seen the ambulances this morning on her way to work. Roaring up Duke Street, their sirens wailing, powering through the busy early morning traffic.

'I wonder what's wrong with Gideon?' Tom continued as he reached for more soap.

She'd hoped he'd given up on the subject, but he obviously hadn't.

'Seasonal affective disorder syndrome, like the rest of us?' she suggested with a smile, but it didn't get her anywhere. In fact, Tom's frown deepened.

'Helen reckons he's got girl trouble, but I can't see how when he's not dating anyone.'

Determinedly Annie continued scrubbing her hands.

'It's not like him,' Tom continued. 'He's usually so easygoing and laid-back, but something's obviously got under his skin.'

Me, according to my brother, she thought ruefully.

'You're a fool, Annie,' he'd said when he'd left on Monday night. 'OK, so Nick hurt you badly, but that was more than four years ago. You've got to forget—move on—and stop running away from any man who shows the least bit of interest in you.'

He was right, she knew he was, but she was scared, so very scared. Yes, she was attracted to Gideon Caldwell, but to let down her guard, allow herself to trust a man again, and not just any man, but another man who was her boss...

She couldn't do it. This time it wouldn't just be her who would get hurt if it all went wrong. This time there was Jamie to consider. If he became fond of Gideon, and Gideon walked away, she would never forgive herself.

'Ready to start, Annie?'

Carol Bannerman's fibroid op, yes, she thought as she followed Tom into the operating theatre. A relationship with Gideon, no. No way.

'Vital signs, Barry?' Tom asked.

'Fine. No problems this end,' the anaesthetist answered.

'OK, let's roll.'

Deftly Tom made several tiny incisions into Carol's abdominal wall to accommodate the laparoscope and other instruments he needed, then ushered Annie forward so she could look inside the woman's uterus.

'As you can see, she has quite a few fibroids, and

they're rather scattered,' he observed, 'but none are unduly large so hopefully electrosurgery will remove them
completely.'

'Would there have been a problem if her fibroids had
been much bigger?' she asked, stepping back to let Tom
begin the delicate task of burning out the fibroids.

'Just the usual ones associated with any kind of surgery—excessive bleeding and infection. Excessive bleeding is certainly more of a danger with very large tumours,
but so long as you have an ample supply of compatible
blood it's not too much of a problem. And avoidance of
infection is generally a matter of good nursing after-care.'

He was an excellent teacher. Quiet, calm and tolerant,
too, of the many questions she asked.

'You're enjoying this, aren't you?' he said with a smile
once Carol's operation was over and Annie had stayed on
to assist him with a bladder repair and then a hysterectomy.

'There's so much to learn,' she said, following him into
the changing room to scrub up again in preparation for
Louise Harper's laparoscopy, 'but, yes. I'm really enjoying it.'

'Perhaps you're meant to be a surgeon,' he commented,
pulling off his soiled theatre top.

It didn't matter if she was, she thought with a slight
sigh. Surgeons worked long and unpredictable hours and,
with Jamie to look after, it really wasn't a serious option.

'It's your suspected PID next, isn't it?' Tom continued.
'Gideon told me you how you managed to persuade
her—' He grimaced as his bleeper went off. 'Sorry, but it
looks like Louise's op is cancelled for this morning.
Nobody bleeps me in Theatre unless it's an emergency.
Could you let Barry know not to prep her?'

Annie nodded but her heart sank as Tom rushed off.
When she'd seen Louise earlier that morning the girl had
already obviously been having second thoughts, and she

dreaded to think what she'd do now. Sign herself out probably, but an emergency always took priority over everything else.

Reluctantly she pulled off her theatre top, and was just about to dump it in the laundry basket when the door of the changing room clattered open.

'Where's Tom?' Gideon demanded.

'I…um…' Oh, cripes, but this is ridiculous, she told herself, all too aware that she was clutching her theatre top to her like some prudish Victorian miss. Gideon had probably seen hundreds—if not thousands—of completely naked women during his career, so the sight of her in a plain white cotton bra was hardly likely to embarrass him. It embarrassed the hell out of her, though. 'His…his bleeper went off. I was—I'm just going—to tell Barry we'll have to cancel Louise's op.'

'Why?'

'Because Tom's gone,' she said in confusion. 'And there's nobody here to perform the operation.'

'I'm a surgeon, aren't I?' he snapped, 'or are you dashing off as usual to pick up your son?'

The unfairness of his remark cut her to the quick. She had never left the hospital early. In fact, the staff at Jamie's day-care centre were becoming very snippy about the number of times she'd arrived late to collect him, but she had no intention of arguing with Gideon, not when he was in this mood. Instead, she pulled a fresh theatre top over her head.

'I'm ready whenever you are, Mr Caldwell.'

For a second he glared at her furiously, then dragged his hands through his already tousled hair. 'Oh, hell, I'm sorry. That was totally uncalled-for, wasn't it? Taking my anger out on you. I'm sorry, Annie, truly sorry.'

And he looked awful, she suddenly realised. His face was drawn and ashen, his eyes red-rimmed with fatigue. Something was clearly very badly wrong, and as she continued to stare at him she also noticed something else. He was wearing theatre scrubs and they were stained with blood.

'The pregnant woman you were operating on,' she said tentatively. 'The one involved in the multiple crash—'

'She made it, the baby didn't.'

His voice was tight, rough, and she half stretched out her hand to him, only to let it fall. 'Gideon, I'm sorry.'

'She was drunk, Annie,' he spat out. 'Half past seven in the morning, eight months pregnant with her unborn child, and driving with her other two kids in the back seat, and she was drunk.'

She stared at him, aghast. 'Her other children—are they all right?'

'Her son has a fractured leg and arm. His two-year-old sister has a fractured skull and major facial lacerations.' He was pacing the changing-room floor now as though he feared that if he stood still too long all the anger within him might explode. 'What kind of woman gets into a car blind drunk, Annie? If she didn't give a damn about herself, you'd think she'd at least have thought about her kids for once.'

'For once… You mean, you think she's been drunk before?'

'The baby I delivered had some of the worst symptoms of foetal alcohol syndrome I've ever seen,' he said grimly. 'Facial deformities, stunted limbs… And do you want to hear something really ironic? Her husband's a GP.'

'He's a doctor?' she gasped. 'But—'

'I know.' He nodded. 'You'd think she, of all people, would know there really is no safe period during which a pregnant woman can drink too much. All the alcohol passes straight across the placental barrier to the foetus.'

'Her husband, does he know—about the baby—her drinking?'

'He does now.' His face twisted. 'It wasn't…pleasant

telling him. He called me a liar, and a lot worse. Swore he'd never seen a drop of alcohol pass her lips, which means either *he's* a liar, or she's damn clever.'

'Oh, Gideon...'

'It's the waste, Annie, the stupid, pointless waste,' he exclaimed bitterly. 'To drink as much as she's obviously been doing for the past eight months—to knowingly harm her own unborn child—that would have been bad enough, but I saw her daughter. Her face—her little face—it's smashed to bits.'

She gazed at him silently. He obviously badly needed somebody to hold him, to comfort him. Do it, her mind whispered. If it was anybody else you wouldn't hesitate for a second, so do it—help him.

Awkwardly she took a step forward, only to come to a halt when the door of the changing room opened and one of the theatre sisters appeared.

'Mr Caldwell, Barry wants to know whether you want Louise Harper prepped, or...?'

He rubbed his hands wearily across his face. 'Five minutes, Sister. Give me five minutes to scrub up, and I'll be with you.'

'Gideon, are you sure about this?' Annie asked, the minute the girl had gone. 'I could page Woody, ask her to—'

'You promised Louise I'd do it, and I'll do it,' he replied, yanking his theatre top off and throwing it into the laundry basket. 'Work is what I need right now, Annie. Not time to think, and brood.'

She badly needed work, too, she thought as she stared at the broad, muscular chest he'd just exposed. That, or a very long, very cold shower.

Oh, for heaven's sake, get a grip, Annie, she told herself. It's a chest. All men have chests. You saw Tom's earlier and it didn't make your heart race, or your breath feel as though it had been sucked right out of your lungs.

But, then, Tom's theatre top hadn't hidden a chest which was covered with a swathe of silky smooth dark hair that disappeared tantalisingly down into the waistband of his theatre trousers. Tom's chest hadn't been anywhere near as broad, or as muscular, or as just plain damn desirable.

'Annie?'

Gideon was gazing at her curiously, and she whirled towards the sink and began scrubbing up as though her very life depended on it. Lord, had he seen her staring at him—realised what she was thinking, feeling? Please, heaven, he hadn't, or she'd never be able to look him in the face again.

'I...I won't be a minute,' she said, trying and failing to keep her voice steady.

He didn't answer and she shot him a swift sidelong glance. Maybe he hadn't actually caught her staring, but he'd obviously seen her blush because he was pulling a fresh theatre top out of the cupboard and dragging it swiftly over his head.

Nick would never have done that. Nick would have taken full advantage of the situation, teased her about the blush, demanded to know what had caused it. Gideon had clearly seen her embarrassment, realised he was the cause—and had immediately done something to rectify it.

Unfortunately.

Oh, pull yourself together, she told herself crossly when Gideon silently began scrubbing up beside her. What's happened to your resolve, your determination never to get involved with a man again, and certainly not with another consultant? One glimpse of a broad, masculine chest and you're falling to bits.

Well, you can jolly well stick yourself back together again, she thought when the theatre sister put her head round the changing-room door to announce that Louise Harper was fully anaesthetised.

She'd have to be insane to let down her guard, no matter how enticing the temptation, and the one thing she wasn't at the moment was insane. Nuts, yes, but insane, no.

It took only a few minutes for Gideon to make the small incision he needed into Louise's abdomen. Quickly he inserted the tiny flexible tube which would allow him to view her internal abdominal and pelvic organs, but as soon as he'd linked it to the video camera and flicked on the monitor screen, he groaned.

'Oh, hell, Annie. Look at this. It's a complete mess.'

It was. All morning she'd been hoping that Louise Harper's PID might be confined to a small, localised area. Right up until the second when Gideon had made the incision into the girl's stomach she'd still been hoping, but the evidence of the video camera was irrefutable. It was bad. Very bad indeed.

'The damage to her Fallopian tubes, and that large abscess on the right side of her uterus—it's got to have been caused by gonorrhoea or chlamydia, hasn't it?' she said.

He nodded. 'Considering the pain she was experiencing when she was brought in, I'd say it was definitely caused by gonorrhoea. With a chlamydial infection there's generally no symptoms at all. I'll take samples to confirm it, of course, and I'd better take some to test for HIV as well.'

'HIV?'

'Annie, you only need to make love with one infected person to catch the disease.'

She knew that, but it would be tough enough telling Louise she had pelvic inflammatory disease. Please God, she didn't have to tell her she was HIV positive as well.

'Look, if she does turn out to be HIV positive, I'll tell her,' Gideon continued as though he'd read her mind, but she shook her head.

'I'll do it. I was the one who talked her into having the laparoscopy, remember?' she said quickly as he opened his mouth to protest. 'And I don't want her thinking I was too chicken to give her the bad news.'

'Chicken' was the last word he'd use to describe Annie Hart, Gideon thought as he drained the abscess in Louise's uterus, then began taking samples from the girl's damaged Fallopian tubes. She was gutsy, and pretty, and a total idiot where men were concerned if Jamie's father was anything to go by.

Lord, but he'd felt such an idiot when he'd stood in her sitting room, clutching those damn flowers, which he'd known had been a mistake. Then he'd been pleased. Of course he had. OK—all right—so maybe initially his heart had contracted in a most puzzling way, but he'd been pleased to discover that she wasn't all alone in the world, that she had somebody to take care of her.

But the more he'd thought about it, the angrier he'd become.

What sort of man allowed the woman he loved—not to mention his own son—to live in a dark, depressing flat where she was constantly harassed by her landlady? What sort of man never offered to help her with her shopping but expected her to drag it home by herself?

It was obvious the man was a jerk. And not just a jerk, but a married jerk, too, he thought grimly, or why else had Annie reacted so furiously when she'd thought *he* was married?

It's none of your business, his mind whispered. Women are fools all the time where men are concerned, so it's none of your business. All you can do is be her friend. Be there if she ever needs help, but otherwise keep out of her life.

Which was what he fully intended doing, so why was he having such trouble forgetting the tantalising glimpse he'd had of a pair of lush, creamy breasts encased in a plain white bra? Why did he suddenly have such an overwhelming desire to go out and punch something, or someone?

'Louise won't ever be able to get pregnant without undergoing IVF treatment, will she?'

Annie's blue eyes were fixed on him above her mask, clearly hoping he would deny it, but he couldn't.

'It's highly unlikely,' he admitted. 'And even with IVF, a woman with a history of PID is ten times more likely to have an ectopic pregnancy.'

'Because her Fallopian tubes are so badly damaged?'

He nodded. 'The fertilised egg can't pass into the uterus to grow. Instead, it attaches itself to the Fallopian tube, and because it can't grow there the pregnancy can be life-threatening to the mother as well as almost always fatal to the foetus.'

She sighed. 'Poor Louise.'

'In a sense she's one of the lucky ones,' he commented, sliding the samples he'd taken into sterile dishes and sealing them. 'At least we've discovered she's got it, and can start treating her.'

Annie doubted very much whether Louise would consider herself lucky as she watched Gideon remove the laparoscopy tube, then insert a few stitches into the incision he'd made. In fact, Louise was undoubtedly going to be devastated.

'I'll finish up here,' Gideon said suddenly. 'It's well past one o'clock. Get yourself down to the canteen and have something to eat.'

'I don't mind waiting.'

He shook his head. 'I'll manage fine, and you look worn out.'

He looked worse, she thought, but the last thing he needed was her arguing with him, so reluctantly she left the theatre, changed out of her scrubs and made her way downstairs. Not to the canteen—she had no appetite for food—but into the staffroom instead.

'You're back late from Theatre,' Rachel Dunwoody said, glancing up at her entrance.

She made it sound like an accusation. Actually, everything that Woody said to her sounded like an accusation. Helen had said it was just the specialist registrar's manner, but it still set Annie's teeth on edge.

'There was a slight hold-up,' she replied as evenly as she could. 'Tom had to shoot off because of an emergency, and it took time for Gideon to scrub up.'

'I heard about the woman he was operating on—the driver involved in the M8 pile-up,' Woody said. 'It was unfortunate.'

'Unfortunate' wasn't the word Annie would have used but she let it pass. 'Do you know anything about the emergency Tom had to go to?' she said instead.

'A major placenta praevia with vaginal bleeding.'

'Is the patient all right—and the baby?' Annie asked, concerned.

'She was thirty-eight weeks pregnant so Tom delivered by Caesarean section. Mother and baby are fine, as far as I know.'

The information didn't appear to give Rachel much pleasure. In fact, she looked depressed. Thinner too, if that was possible, with dark shadows under her eyes. If it had been Helen or Liz, Annie would immediately have asked what was wrong, but the specialist registrar wasn't the kind of woman who invited confidences. She wasn't the kind of woman who invited conversation, full stop, and it was a guilty relief to Annie when she finally left.

Her relief, however, was short-lived. Just when she was trying to make up her mind whether to make herself a piece of toast or not, Liz appeared, looking worried.

'Annie, sorry to interrupt your break, but Kay Wilson hasn't eaten any of her lunch, and she says she's not hungry.'

Annie's eyebrows shot up. 'Not hungry?'

'That's what I thought,' Liz said with an uncertain laugh. 'I mean, normally Kay considers anything less than half a haunch of lamb for lunch a mere snack, but today…'

'Did she eat any breakfast?' Annie asked, putting down her mug.

The sister shook her head. 'She said she felt a bit queasy, but that could be because of the chicken curry her husband smuggled in to her last night.'

'He smuggled a chicken curry into the ward?' Annie said in disbelief as she followed Liz out of the staffroom.

'I know.' Liz chuckled. 'You'd think the idiot would have realised the smell would carry, wouldn't you?'

A bubble of laughter sprang to Annie's lips. At the Manchester Infirmary it had been quite common for husbands and partners to smuggle in fish and chips in for their loved ones, but a chicken curry?

'What's this I hear about you refusing our superb hospital food?' she asked as Liz closed the curtains round Kay's bed.

The young woman managed a weak smile. 'I don't seem to feel very hungry today, Doctor.'

'Nothing to do with the chicken curry you had last night, I suppose?' Annie observed, her eyes dancing.

'No—at least I don't think so. I just, well, I just don't feel very great somehow.'

That was unusual, too. Kay had been the life and soul of the ward since she'd had her baby. In fact, it had been virtually impossible to get her to rest when it had finally been confirmed that the high levels of sugar present in her urine during her pregnancy had been caused by her fluctuating hormone levels and not because she'd developed diabetes.

'I'd like to take a quick look at you, Kay,' she said.

'Must you?' the girl protested. 'I'm fine. Just a bit itchy down below.'

'Itchy?' Annie repeated. 'What sort of itchy?'

'How many kinds of itchy are there?' Kay said irritably. 'I'm just itchy, and my legs—my legs feel like lead weights.'

Annie nodded to Liz but when the sister swiftly pulled down the bedclothes and rolled up Kay's nightdress it was all Annie could do not to gasp out loud. Kay's breasts were red and inflamed, and so was her vagina.

Puerperal fever. It was rare—very rare in Western countries—but it did happen. A mother who had experienced a long labour and lost a lot of blood, as Kay had done during her son's birth, had a greatly reduced defence mechanism. Any raw surfaces provided easy access to micro-organisms, and especially to the bacterium streptococcus haemolyticus.

'I'm afraid I need to take some more blood samples and swabs from you, Kay,' she declared with a calmness she was very far from feeling.

'Doctor, I already feel like a pin cushion after all those samples you took when my baby was born,' Kay exclaimed.

'Hopefully, these will be the last,' Annie said soothingly, 'and I'll be as fast as I can, I promise.'

She just prayed the lab would be as quick to test them. If Kay did have puerperal fever they had to get on top of it immediately. Left unchecked it could spread to the surrounding lymph ducts and veins, causing abscesses, peritonitis, deep-vein thrombosis and even septicaemia.

'Well spotted,' Gideon commented, when Kay's blood results came back from the lab confirming Annie's diagnosis. 'Puerperal fever's not the kind of thing most doctors expect to come across nowadays in Britain.'

'I can't take any credit,' Annie replied, embarrassed by his praise. 'It was Liz who noticed she wasn't eating.'

'Yes, but you had the foresight to immediately send off

blood samples, thereby saving valuable time. We've got a blood transfusion started, and an IV line of penicillin, so with luck we should be able to knock it on the head before it has a chance to spread. And speaking of samples,' he continued as they walked down the ward together, 'Louise's results are back from the lab.'

'And?' she asked, not really wanting to know.

'The good news is she tested negative for HIV. The bad news is the damage to her Fallopian tubes was definitely caused by gonorrhoea. We need to get her started immediately on intravenous antibiotics—at least two different kinds to really give this thing a double whammy.'

'What about her boyfriend?' she said, her heart sinking. 'He's going to need treatment, too, isn't he?'

'As will her previous boyfriend. Look, I'll speak to her, Annie,' he continued, clearly sensing her dismay. 'It's too much to expect—'

'I said I'd tell her, and I will,' she interrupted, but her talk with Louise turned out to be one of the worst forty-five minutes of Annie's medical career.

'Nothing I said made it any better—nothing I said helped,' she sadly told Gideon in his room later.

'I don't believe that for a minute,' he protested. 'I've seen you with patients, and you're good.'

'But she's still got PID,' she murmured, and he sighed.

'Annie, we're not magicians, or gods. We can't wave a magic wand and make everybody better, or eradicate the need to break unwelcome news. At least we can treat Louise—cure her infection. OK, so her Fallopian tubes are badly damaged, but she's still alive, she has a future, and it was your powers of persuasion which gave her that.'

'I…I guess so,' she said, clearly unconvinced, and he smiled.

'You're just like my wife. She wanted to cure the whole world, too.'

What could she say? 'I'm sorry she died' sounded so inadequate, but to say nothing...

'She sounds like she was a very nice lady,' she said hesitantly.

'Yes. Yes, she was.' He picked up a file from his desk, then put it down again. 'Susan didn't get the chance you've given Louise. I didn't know she had ovarian cancer until it was too late, you see. It was ironic, really. I got promoted to consultant just after we were married, and yet I didn't know.'

'Nobody could have,' she exclaimed, seeing the pain and heartache in his face. 'Ovarian cancer—it's such a horrible, insidious disease, with so few symptoms...'

'I know.' His face tightened. 'I know, but...it doesn't help.'

'Gideon—'

'Good heavens, is it four o'clock already?' he exclaimed with a forced brightness that tugged at her heart. 'You'd better get your skates on or Jamie will think you're lost.'

He was right—Jamie would—but she didn't want to leave him like this, looking so lost, suddenly so very lonely.

'I'm not in any great rush,' she lied. 'Especially when Mrs Patterson will undoubtedly be waiting for me with her latest list of complaints.'

'Would you like me to talk to her again—more tactfully this time?' he offered. 'Or how about if I ask around the hospital—see if anybody on the staff has a flat to rent?'

She shook her head. 'I'm afraid Jamie would be noisy wherever we lived. What he really needs is to get out more, to run off some of his high spirits.'

'Why don't you take him to the Botanic Gardens?' he suggested. 'There's long walks, short walks...'

'I know. I used to take him there a lot in his pram when

I lived in Hyndland, but it's too far to walk from Thornton Street, and the buses are a nightmare.'

'Couldn't David…?' Gideon gritted his teeth. Lord, simply saying the man's name was enough to make him angry, but he was going to be calm if it killed him. 'Couldn't he drive you to the park?'

'He takes us out as often as he can, but he's really busy right now, and I don't like to impose on him when he's got his own life to lead,' she said without thinking.

Heaven give me strength, Gideon thought furiously. So David has his own life to lead, has he? Was Annie terminally stupid, or just so much in love that she couldn't see the jerk was using her?

'What sort of work keeps him so busy?' he demanded.

'He's a specialist registrar in obs and gynae at the Merkland Memorial.'

An obs and gynae specialist registrar who had clearly never heard of condoms or responsibility, Gideon thought savagely.

Well, he was not going to lose his temper. He was not going to tell her she was a fool, but he was going to say something whether she liked it or not.

'I'd have thought even a busy specialist registrar could have spared the odd afternoon to take his son to the park.'

A slow flush of uncomfortable colour spread across Annie's cheeks. For a second she'd forgotten that Gideon thought David was Jamie's father. Well, she had two choices. She could tell him the truth or she could allow him to go on believing the lie.

It's better if he believes the lie, a part of her insisted. It's safer, remember?

Yes, but it wasn't better. One lie would become another, then another, and this was a nice man, a genuine man. To lie to him would be unforgivable.

'David…' She cleared her throat. 'David isn't Jamie's father. He's my brother.'

'Your brother?' he echoed faintly.

'Didn't I introduce him when you came round?' she said brightly, praying she wouldn't be struck down for the lie. 'I thought I did.'

'No—no, you didn't.'

He looked slightly dazed, but at least he didn't look quite so depressed any more, and she reached for her handbag. 'I'd better be going.'

'I could take Jamie to the Botanic Gardens. No, listen,' Gideon continued, when she stared at him, open-mouthed. 'We're both off duty tomorrow so why couldn't we all go then?'

He couldn't be serious—he couldn't possibly be serious—but it seemed he was.

'No—really,' she floundered. 'I couldn't ask you to do that.'

'You didn't. I'm volunteering.'

'But…but what if you're needed at the hospital?' she said, clutching at straws.

'Annie, even consultants are allowed days off, but if it will set your mind at rest I'll take my bleeper with me so if there's a sudden mass outbreak of obstetric or gynaecological emergencies the hospital can contact me.'

'It could rain—or snow,' she offered as a last-ditch stand.

'Then we'll take him to the Burrell Collection and he can run up and down until we're thrown out for creating a disturbance. Annie, quit with the "what ifs", and just give me a simple yes or no, OK?'

Jamie would love it—she knew he would. The trouble was, she would like it as well, which gave her a very good reason to say no.

But why should she say no? All right, so she'd vowed never to get involved with a man again, but going to the park with Gideon wasn't getting involved.

It depends on what it leads to, her mind whispered, and a disconcerting shiver ran down her spine.

'Annie, if you're worried about upsetting me or hurting my feelings by saying no, there's no need.'

She glanced up at him. He was expecting her to refuse. He looked tired, and resigned, and just a little sad, and suddenly she knew she didn't want to refuse.

'We'd love to come.'

'Y-you would?'

An involuntary chuckle broke from her at his stunned expression. 'You can take back your invitation if you want to.'

'Of course I don't want to. I just— I mean, I didn't…' A broad smile lit up his face. 'That's great. Really great. I'll pick you up at ten-thirty tomorrow, then, shall I? We don't want to get to the gardens too late—not with there being so little daylight at this time of year. And why don't we have lunch in one of the cafés near the park afterwards? I'm sure Jamie would love it, and then after lunch…'

After lunch? Annie thought as Gideon launched into a list of the things they might possibly do in the afternoon. How had a simple trip to the park suddenly turned into a full-day expedition?

'Gideon—'

'Just leave everything to me, Annie,' he said firmly. 'All you have to do is be ready on time.'

He was wrong, she thought as she stared up at him. The most important thing was for her to keep remembering that he was a friend, nothing more, or tomorrow was going to turn out to be one of the biggest mistakes of her life.

CHAPTER FIVE

THE sky was blue, there wasn't a cloud in the sky and even the hint of frost Annie had seen earlier, glinting on the rooftops had disappeared. It was a perfect day for the Botanic Gardens.

In fact, it was a perfect day to go anywhere that didn't have her brother in the vicinity, Annie decided as he launched into yet another whistled rendition of 'Can't help falling in love'.

'David, if you dropped by with the sole purpose of winding me up, I'd far rather you just left,' she declared in exasperation.

He opened his eyes very wide. 'Winding you up? Can't a bloke whistle if he feels like it?'

She scowled at him, then leapt forward with a warning cry to retrieve Jamie who was wobbling precariously on the back of an armchair, trying to look out of the window.

'Jamie, if I've told you once, I've told you a hundred times, Mr Caldwell will be here when the big hand is at six and the little hand is at ten,' she exclaimed.

'But he is coming today, isn't he, Mummy?' her son asked, his small face worried, uncertain. 'We really are going to the park, aren't we?'

Her throat tightened as she stared down at him. He'd been up since six o'clock this morning, full of excitement, bursting with enthusiasm, and it was for so very little. A simple trip to the park, that was all, but to Jamie a day out was as thrilling and unusual as a visit to the moon.

'All working mums feel the same, love,' her brother

murmured, clearly reading her mind. 'Don't start mentally beating yourself up, thinking you're neglecting him.'

It was easy for him to say, but how could she not feel guilty? How could she not sometimes wonder in the dark lonely hours of the night whether she should give up her dream of becoming a specialist registrar and settle instead for some part-time medical work? Work that would give her more free time with Jamie.

'You could always move back in with me if you're finding things tough,' David continued, his eyes fixed on her.

For a second she was tempted, then her lips curved and she shook her head. 'And cramp your style with all your lovely ladies—what kind of sister would that make me?'

'My kid sister, and I worry about you.'

His voice was uncharacteristically gruff, and she gazed at him in dismay. 'David, I'm fine—truly I am. OK, so maybe sometimes I get a bit down-wonder if I'm doing the right thing by Jamie—but, please, don't worry about me. I really am all right.'

He gazed at her thoughtfully. 'I guess you must be if you've started dating again.'

'Gideon and I aren't dating,' she exclaimed, annoyingly aware that she was blushing. 'As I told you on the phone, he's simply taking Jamie and me to the park. It's no big deal.'

Her brother's eyes drifted over her. 'No big deal, huh? So how come you're not wearing your normal Saturday morning outfit—those tatty old jogging pants and that baggy sweatshirt?'

Her colour deepened. OK, so perhaps she'd made a bit of an effort this morning by putting on her last decent pair of corduroy trousers and topping them with a fluffy green sweater, and she'd washed her hair last night, but that was only because she didn't want Gideon to be embarrassed in her company.

'You were the one who said I should get out more,' she said irrationally. 'You were the one who said—'

'Hey, don't get your knickers in a twist,' he protested. 'If you say it's not a date, it's not a date. Which means you won't mind if I stick around until he gets here, check him out?'

'Check him out?' she spluttered. 'David, don't you dare. Not if you want to leave this flat walking.'

Her front doorbell rang and her brother glanced down at his watch. 'Ten twenty-five. My word, he's keen.'

'David.'

'Sweetness and light, little sister.' He beamed. 'I'll be nothing but sweetness and light.'

Which was enough to scare the hell out of anybody, Annie thought as she went to let Gideon in.

'Am I too early?' Gideon said, clearly misinterpreting her expression. 'The traffic wasn't as heavy as I'd thought it would be.'

'No, of course you're not too early,' she reassured him. 'I just have to collect one or two things.'

'He's been here before.' Jamie had followed her down the hall, and was surveying Gideon with a mixture of curiosity and uncertainty. 'Is he the one who's taking us to the park?'

'That's right.' Gideon smiled, crouching down to Jamie's height. 'My name's Gideon, and I'm a friend of your mummy's.'

'Mummy said you're a doctor like her,' Jamie observed, 'but that you were the big cheese.'

Annie's eyes flew to Gideon's in embarrassed consternation, but to her relief he grinned.

'Any particular type or flavour?' he asked, his brown eyes brimming with laughter.

'Stilton, perhaps.' She chuckled. 'Or how about Brie? Crusty on the outside, but soft as butter in the middle.'

'Or Danish blue,' her brother declared, appearing beside them without warning. 'Which can cause severe allergic reactions in people who can't take penicillin.'

Gideon straightened up. He was half a head taller than David but in Annie's small hallway he looked even bigger. 'You're Annie's brother.'

'You're Annie's boss.'

'And David's just leaving, aren't you, David?' Annie said quickly, glancing from her brother to Gideon with foreboding.

'I'm not in any rush,' David replied. 'In fact, why don't you go and collect Jamie's emergency travelling gear while Gideon and I become better acquainted?'

'Jamie's emergency travelling gear?' Gideon repeated, clearly puzzled.

'I always takes a spare set of Jamie's underpants and trousers with me whenever we go anywhere,' Annie explained. 'He sometimes gets a bit excited, you see, and forgets to ask to go.'

'You should be taking notes, Gideon,' David said. 'For future dates.'

'David.'

Her brother smiled. 'Just trying to be helpful, sis.'

Yeah, right, she thought, but this kind of help she could do without. 'I won't be a minute, Gideon,' she said, shooting her brother a glance which said, Don't you dare to interrogate Gideon or make any smart remarks.

'We'll wait for you in the sitting room,' David replied with a grin that said, Hey, what do you take me for? It didn't reassure her for a second as she shot down the corridor, towing a loudly protesting Jamie behind her.

'Annie tells me you're a specialist registrar at the

Merkland Memorial,' Gideon said, as he followed David into the sitting room.

'That's right. Annie told me you're taking her and Jamie to the Botanic Gardens.'

'That's right.'

'Hoping to strike lucky with my sister, are you?'

Gideon's eyes narrowed. 'As you're Annie's brother I'll let that pass. If you'd been anybody else I'd have punched you on the nose.'

'Fair enough.' David nodded. 'But Annie's my kid sister—'

'Then why do you let her live in this dump?'

'I don't *let* Annie do anything,' David replied, his voice tight. 'My sister makes her own decisions—always has. Getting her to stay with me when she was pregnant was tough. Persuading her to stay on after Jamie was born was even harder. She wanted her independence, and she wanted her own flat. I tried to talk her out of both, she said no.'

'I see.'

'I don't think you do—not yet—but you will.'

'David—'

'Annie tells me you're a widower. Is that true?'

Gideon's eyebrows rose. 'Do you want to see my wife's death certificate?'

'It would be reassuring.'

'Now, just a minute—'

'Annie hasn't had an easy life,' David interrupted, 'and I don't just mean these past four years. Our parents were killed in a car crash when she was sixteen and I was twenty. We were left with no money, and it was Annie who washed dishes after school so I could complete my medical training, Annie who took a weekend job in a supermarket to feed us both.'

'I know she's special—'

'So do I, which is why I want to make one thing crystal clear. If you ever hurt my sister—make her unhappy—I'll make you wish you'd never been born.'

'David—'

'Everything OK in here?' Annie asked, red-cheeked and breathless as she dashed into the sitting room, clutching a carrier bag, with Jamie at her side.

David smiled. 'Everything's hunky-dory. In fact, I think Gideon and I understand one another perfectly now.'

She didn't like the sound of that at all, but there was no time to ask for an explanation. Not when Jamie was already heading excitedly for the door and Gideon was following him with his car seat, but she turned to him anxiously as they drove away from Thornton Street.

'I hope David didn't say anything to upset you. He means well, but sometimes he forgets I'm not eighteen any more.'

'He didn't upset me in the least,' Gideon replied smoothly.

'He was the same when I was a teenager,' she continued. 'Always fussing over me, grilling every boyfriend I ever had. It was one of the reasons why I opted to go down south to do my medical studies.'

In the light of what had obviously happened to her down south she might have been better—safer—to have stayed in Glasgow, Gideon thought ruefully, but he didn't say that.

'Annie, it's OK,' he said instead. 'Nothing David said annoyed or angered me.'

She had to be content with that. Jamie was already clamouring to know if they'd reached the park yet, and she took solace in the fact that Gideon didn't appear to be unduly ruffled. Which didn't mean, of course, that she wasn't going to give her brother merry hell the next time she saw him. His constant interrogation of her boyfriends had been bad enough when she'd been eighteen, but she sure as heck wasn't going to let him get away with it now she was twenty-eight.

Not that Gideon was a boyfriend, of course, she told herself firmly. He was a friend, nothing more, but that still didn't mean she liked the idea of her brother grilling him.

Especially when Gideon proved to be both an entertaining and informative companion in the gardens.

'How did you get to know so much about the eating habits of squirrels?' she asked in admiration as they strolled along the path, with Jamie running ahead of them. 'Not to mention being able to identify every tree.'

'My grandfather used to take my brother and me out to Loch Lomond every weekend,' Gideon replied, 'and there was nothing Grandpa Caldwell didn't know about the countryside.'

'Is your brother a doctor, too?' she asked, and he laughed.

'Heavens, no. Richard was the sensible one. He became a lawyer and earns considerably more than I do for working a lot fewer hours.'

'Would you swap if you could?' she said curiously, and he smiled and shook his head.

'Not in a million years. I love my job. In fact, it's my whole life now.'

But it shouldn't be, she thought with a slight frown as she watched him swing Jamie up into his arms so he could see a squirrel sitting on the branch above them. He should have more—he deserved more. He should have a wife, and children of his own.

He could have you, her heart suddenly whispered. He could have you, and Jamie.

Definitely not, her mind shrieked, absolutely not. You're never going to get involved with a man again,

remember. It's just you and Jamie against the world, remember.

But you like him, don't you? her heart whispered when
Gideon gently lowered Jamie to the ground. You like him
a lot.

She did. Actually, it was odd, but she'd never once
asked herself whether she liked Nick. Oh, she'd loved
him—loved him desperately—but she'd never once asked
herself whether she *liked* him.

'Mummy, what's that big building over there?' Jamie
demanded. 'The glass one?'

'It's the Kibble Palace,' she answered, dragging her
thoughts back to the present with difficulty. 'An engineer
called John Kibble built it a long time ago as a conser-
vatory—a sort of big greenhouse—for his home at Loch
Long. He gave it to the Royal Botanic Institution in 1873
and they dismantled it, then shipped it up the Clyde and
rebuilt it here.'

'Can we go inside?'

'Of course we can,' she replied, and with a whoop of
delight Jamie was off and running towards the entrance.

'He seems to be enjoying himself.' Gideon laughed.

'So am I,' she admitted. 'I'd forgotten how lovely the
gardens were.'

'Have you ever been here in the summer for one of
their open-air concerts?'

She shook her head. 'I always meant to come when I
was younger, but somehow I never got around to it.'

'Then we'll certainly have to rectify that,' he declared
as he led the way into the palace. 'I'll bring you here in
the summer.'

It sounded magical. A concert in the open air, on a
balmy summer's evening, with a full moon shining, and
Gideon at her side. It sounded…romantic.

And you're doing it again, she thought with dismay—

thinking about him as a man, and not simply as a friend. Good grief, woman, you haven't even a clue how he feels about you. OK, so he's brought you and Jamie here for the day, but that doesn't mean anything. He could be bored out of his skull right this minute, and you wouldn't know it.

But he doesn't look bored, she argued back. Look at him talking to Jamie, listening to what he's saying. Does that look like a bored man to you? No, but, then, he wouldn't allow his boredom to show, she thought with a slight sigh. He was that sort of man.

'Mummy—Mummy, come and see,' Jamie said excitedly, grabbing her by the arm. 'There's a pond in here, and it has huge goldfish in it.'

Obediently she allowed him drag her towards it. 'I think they're carp, sweetheart.' She frowned. 'If they're not, they're pretty beefy goldfish.'

'Carp for sure.' Gideon nodded, tugging at his shirt collar. 'Phew, I'd forgotten how hot it is in here.'

'It's for the palm trees, sir,' one of the gardeners said, overhearing him. 'We keep the air hot and humid to mimic a rainforest.'

'Well, it certainly feels like one,' a teenager with a baby in her arms observed, looking distinctly harassed as she passed them.

Gideon shook his head as he watched the girl leave the palace. 'Look at her, Annie. She can't be a day over sixteen and yet already she's saddled with a child. And there's no need for it nowadays. Not with so many forms of birth control available.'

'I guess not.'

Something in Annie's voice made him glance round at her quickly, and what he saw in her face brought a wave of hot colour to his cheeks. 'Annie, I'm not implying that you—I'm not suggesting that you—'

'It's all right,' she said quietly. 'I didn't want or plan to be a single parent either, but unfortunately the Pill isn't always a hundred per cent effective.'

He stared at the palm trees silently for a second, then cleared his throat. 'Annie, I don't want you to take this the wrong way—I mean, your son is a joy and a delight— but being a single parent, it can't have been easy, and—'

'You're wondering why I didn't have a termination.' She sighed. 'I probably would have if I'd known earlier that I was pregnant. I was twenty-four years old, I'd just finished my medical degree and the last thing I needed was a baby, but I didn't know I was pregnant until I was twenty-two weeks. My menstrual cycle has always been pretty erratic, you see, and I was still getting some spotting even at twenty-five weeks.'

'When you found out, you could still have gone ahead,' he observed, his eyes on her, curious, thoughtful. 'Terminations can be carried out even at that late stage.'

'I know, but...' Unconsciously her face softened. 'I'd felt him move. If I hadn't felt him move—realised he was there, that he was real...' She laughed a little shakily. 'That probably sounds really dumb and stupid to you.'

'No. No, it doesn't,' he said huskily. 'I...' He paused, then started again. 'Jamie's father—he's married, isn't he?'

For a second she hesitated, then suddenly it was important that he should know, understand. 'I didn't know he was married, not at first. We met at the Manchester Infirmary—'

'He's a doctor?'

'He was a consultant, and I thought he was single, like me. He didn't tell me he was married until after I fell in love with him, and then he said he was separated, getting a divorce.'

'I take it he wasn't.'

She shook her head as the memories came flooding back. Memories she'd spent four years trying to forget. 'I found out later that he didn't have any intention of getting a divorce. His wife has very good connections, you see—and Nick is a very ambitious man. All he wanted from me was some extra-marital sex.'

'Oh, Annie.'

He'd reached out and grasped her hands tightly in his, and she managed a tiny, lopsided smile. 'Go on—say it. Annie Hart, you were a fool.'

'You loved him, and you thought he loved you,' he said firmly. 'He was the fool to let you go. You're spunky, and brave, and don't let anyone ever tell you otherwise.'

She didn't need them to. She already knew how big a fool she'd been. She only needed to remember the day Nick had told her it was all over between them. When he'd said he wasn't good enough for her, that he wasn't being fair to her, and a month later she'd discovered he'd been having an affair with one of the nurses in Orthopaedics.

'Does he keep in touch with you?' Gideon asked. 'Visit Jamie often?'

Nick doesn't even know I have a child, she thought bitterly. When he left I never wanted to see him again. I still don't.

'And what about financial support?' Gideon continued. 'I'm sure he's legally bound—'

'Can we drop the subject, please, Gideon?' she said quickly. 'I really don't want to talk about it any more.'

'But—'

'Mummy, can we go into some of the other glass houses now?' Jamie interrupted, having got bored with the Kibble Palace.

Annie smiled down at her son with an effort. 'Of course

you can, sweetheart. Which would you like to see first? The fern house, the cactus house, or the exotic plant house?'

Jamie frowned. 'What's an eggotic plant?'

'A plant that comes from a far-away country,' Gideon explained. 'Places like South America, Africa, and India.'

'Effelants come from Africa, don't they?' Jamie exclaimed, his blue eyes lighting up. 'Will we see some effelants?'

'I'm afraid not,' Gideon declared solemnly, 'but you'll see something called a Venus fly-trap which is almost as good.'

Jamie obviously thought it was, too, when he saw it.

'Children are terrible little ghouls, aren't they?' Annie chuckled as her son watched in wide-eyed fascination while one of the gardeners demonstrated how the Venus fly-trap caught its prey.

'I don't think they're so much ghouls as innocent of reality,' Gideon observed. 'We know the fly's being eaten, but to them it's just exciting to see the flower snap shut. And speaking of eating, I think we should start making tracks for lunch or we're never going to get in anywhere.'

He was right. In fact, to Annie's consternation, the only place that wasn't completely full was a small café which only served fish and chips, hamburgers and chips, or eggs and chips.

'I'm sorry about this,' she said as soon as Gideon had ordered. 'I know it's probably not what you're used to—'

'Who says?' He grinned. 'I love hamburgers.'

'And chips?' Jamie asked.

'Absolutely.' Gideon nodded.

'With or without tomato ketchup?' Jamie demanded.

'With—and lots of it,' Gideon replied, winking across at Annie, and she laughed and shook her head.

Nick wouldn't have said that. Nick wouldn't have come

in here in the first place, or cheerfully ordered hamburgers and chips. He'd have considered it beneath his dignity.

'What?' Gideon asked curiously, seeing her smile.

'I'm just thinking what a very nice man you are,' she said.

His grin reappeared. 'Flattery will get you everywhere.'

'No, I mean it,' she insisted. 'Taking Jamie and me to the park—'

'We're going back there again after lunch,' her son piped up. 'To the play park this time.'

'Since when?' Annie asked in surprise.

'Gideon said we were.'

She glanced across at Gideon, who had the grace to look shamefaced.

'Well, he seems really keen to go, Annie, and—'

'In other words he's twisted you round his little finger.' She chuckled. 'OK, we'll go back to the park, but if you're bored out of your skull, don't blame me.'

He wouldn't be bored, Gideon thought when the waitress brought them their hamburgers and chips. How could he be bored with Jamie, and with a girl who was warm, and gentle, and...?

What in the world was happening to him? he wondered as he suddenly realised that his eyes were tracing the smooth outline of Annie's cheek, and his fingers were itching to do the same. Just four short weeks ago his life had been ordered, settled. He'd had his work, his career, and that was all he'd wanted, and then a golden-haired girl with large blue eyes had cannoned into him on the hospital staircase, torn his character to shreds, and nothing had been the same.

Because you're falling in love with her, a little voice whispered at the back of his mind, and he crushed the voice down quickly. It wasn't true—couldn't be true. He liked his life the way it was. No emotional entanglements, no potential for heartache, and yet...

Annie was blowing on Jamie's chips to cool them, and all Gideon could think was how wonderful it would be to turn her head, to capture those lips with his own and taste them. When she stretched across the table to retrieve the salt, and her green fluffy sweater tightened across her breasts, outlining and defining them, all he wanted was to slide his hands beneath that sweater, to touch and caress her.

Sex, he told himself firmly. These thoughts—these feelings—they don't mean anything except that your hormones have kicked into life, and in a big way.

But it wasn't just sex, he realised with dismay when Annie laughed at something Jamie had said, then turned to him to share the joke. Yes, he wanted to hold her, to touch her, but he also knew that he never wanted to let her go.

And it was wrong. How could he have fallen in love with another woman after Susan? He'd adored her. Loved everything about her—her vibrancy, her laughter, her joy.

But Susan's dead, his heart murmured when their lunch was over and they walked back to the park. All the longing and the wanting in the world was never going to bring her back, so maybe it was time he moved on. He would never ever forget her, but maybe...maybe it was time to let her go.

'Mummy, why are all those people having their pictures taken?' Jamie demanded, as they walked past the old physic garden on their way to the play park.

'It's a wedding party,' she explained. 'They've probably had their reception in the Grosvenor Hotel, and have come across here to have their pictures taken because it's such a pretty spot.'

A cheer went up from the party as the groom enthusiastically kissed the bride, and Gideon smiled. 'They look happy.'

'They do,' she agreed, and he took his courage in his hands and asked the question he'd been wanting to ask since lunchtime.

'Would you ever contemplate getting married yourself?'

She shook her head as Jamie dashed into the play park. 'I have my son, and he's all I want in my life.'

'But what about you?' Gideon protested. 'What's going to happen to you when he grows up? He'll want a life of his own, and you'll be all alone.'

'Hopefully, I'll have a career like you by then.' She smiled. 'And you don't appear to have found it lonely.'

He hadn't until now. 'Annie—'

'I don't ever want to fall in love again, Gideon,' she said, her eyes fixed on Jamie as he shot down the slide, then scampered round to the steps to do it again. 'You give your heart, your soul, and it gets trampled in the mud. It's too painful when it ends. Surely you, of all people, must agree with that?'

He thought for a long moment. 'No, I can't say I wish I'd never fallen in love with Susan. When she died…' A muscle tightened in his jaw, and he swallowed, hard. 'When she died, I wanted to die, too. It hurt for a very long time, but she was such a joy, such a delight, I wouldn't want not to have experienced that.'

'It's different for you,' she murmured, watching Jamie whiz down the slide again. 'She didn't leave you willingly. She didn't walk away.'

'All men won't walk away, Annie. Some of us want commitment.'

She sighed. 'Perhaps, but it's not a risk I'm prepared to take.'

'Annie—'

'Mummy, there's a river down there with some ducks in it,' Jamie exclaimed, running up to her excitedly. 'Can we go down and feed them?'

She shook her head. 'It's getting late, sweetheart. I think we'd better start heading for home.'

'Could we go back to the palace, then?' he demanded. 'Look at the big goldfish again?'

'I think you've done more than enough for today,' she said firmly. 'The gardens won't go away, you know,' she added as he stuck out his bottom lip truculently. 'We can always come back another day.'

'With Gideon?'

'Certainly with me,' Gideon replied, before Annie could say anything. 'I want to feed the ducks, too.'

Annie chuckled. 'You're a glutton for punishment, aren't you?'

'I just enjoy the company.'

His voice was unexpectedly deep, husky, and as she glanced up at him she saw a gentleness in his face, a tenderness she'd never seen before. A tenderness that made her mouth feel dry and her heart skitter against her ribcage, and instinctively she took a step back.

'Gideon, don't,' she whispered through a throat so tight it hurt. 'Please...please, don't.'

'Oh, lass, don't you know I would never hurt you?' he said softly.

'You might not want to, or mean to, but...' She shook her head. 'I don't want this. I don't want to be hurt again. I couldn't bear it.'

He reached out and captured her face in his hands. Hands that were big, and warm, and infinitely comforting,

'Never, do you hear me?' he murmured. 'Never will I ever hurt you.'

And to prove his point he bent his head and gently brushed her lips with his own.

It was all he'd intended doing. A simple kiss to prove to her that she had nothing to fear from him. But as soon as his lips touched hers a wave of longing flooded through him, a longing and a desire he hadn't felt in years.

It was like coming home. Like finding the other half of himself he'd been so sure had died with Susan. Did Annie feel it, too, this strange sense of rightness, of belonging? Gideon didn't know. All he knew was that his heart twisted and contracted inside him when he heard her small wistful sigh as his tongue slid gently into her mouth, and he groaned as he felt her body yielding and moulding to his own.

He had to pull away eventually to breathe, but he didn't let go of her. Instead, he leant his forehead against hers, and laughed a little shakily. 'Hell's teeth, that was meant to be a light, friendly kiss, and then…'

'I know,' she gasped, looking every bit as dazed as he felt. 'Goodness knows what Jamie must think.' She looked round him, then behind her, and he felt her stiffen. 'Gideon, where is he? He was right beside us a minute ago.'

'He'll be on the slide again,' he said reassuringly, but he wasn't.

'Gideon, where *is* he?' she cried, her voice rising in pitch as they stared at the empty playground, then at the gardens behind them.

'Calm down, calm down,' he said, though in truth his own heart was none too steady now either. 'He's only four—he can't have gone very far.'

'But the River Kelvin's down there, and there's a gate out to the road. What if he's got onto the road?'

'Annie—'

'Jamie!' she shouted at the top of her voice, but heard nothing but the wind blowing through the trees.

Frantically she shielded her eyes against the setting sun.

There were so many places Jamie could be—trees he could be hiding behind, bushes that were small enough to conceal him—but it was going to be dark soon. What would they do if it got dark?

'Perhaps we should split up,' Gideon suggested, reading her mind. 'I could go towards the river, and you could go back down towards the glasshouses.'

'I don't know—I don't know what to do for the best,' she said, her voice breaking on a sob.

'Look, there's that girl with the baby—the one we saw in the Kibble Palace this morning,' Gideon exclaimed. 'Maybe she's seen him.'

She had.

'I thought it was strange, him being all on his own like that,' she declared, 'but then I thought—'

'Where did you see him?' Annie interrupted impatiently.

'Down by the cactus house. He was talking to a man.'

Oh, dear lord, no, Annie thought as she began to run. Not that. Please, oh, please, not that. She'd warned Jamie time and time again about talking to strangers, of never going anywhere without asking her first, but it was difficult to know how much had sunk in. She hadn't wanted to frighten him, but maybe she should have.

'It's probably just one of the gardeners, Annie,' Gideon said as he ran along beside her. 'Or a park guard.'

But what if it wasn't? She should never have come here, should never have taken her eyes off Jamie for a second. It was all her fault. If anything had happened to him, it was all her fault.

'There he is, Annie,' Gideon suddenly yelled, pointing ahead of him. 'There he is beside the exotic house, and it's all right, he's talking to one of the gardeners.'

He was, and a wave of relief washed over her. Relief which was very quickly superseded by anger.

'How many times have I told you *never* to wander away from me?' she cried, clutching Jamie to her, then giving him a shake. 'You are *never* coming to this park again, do you hear me? *Never!*'

'Annie, he knows he was in the wrong,' Gideon murmured as large tears began to trickle down Jamie's cheeks. 'He knows he shouldn't have wandered off. Don't be too hard on him—'

'Keep out of this, Gideon,' she retorted. 'He's *my* son, not yours, and I decide what he does and doesn't do.'

'Yes, but—'

'Will you take us home, please?'

He did—there was nothing else he could do—but when he drew his car to a halt outside Thornton Street and began to get out, Annie put her hand on his arm to stop him.

'I'd rather you didn't come in, if you don't mind. Jamie and I—we're both very tired.'

'But—'

'It's been a long day, Gideon.'

She was slipping away from him. He could see it in her face, in the way she wasn't quite meeting his eyes. She was closing the door on any hope of a relationship between them, re-erecting the barriers she'd let fall for those all too brief moments in the gardens.

'Annie, just because Jamie wandered off for a few minutes—'

'He wouldn't have wandered off at all if I hadn't allowed myself to be distracted,' she said flatly. 'It was my fault, and it won't happen again.'

'What do you mean, it won't happen again?' he said, though in truth he suspected he already knew the answer. 'Annie, I want to go out with you again. We could take Jamie to the Burrell Collection next Saturday—'

'I'm on duty next Saturday.'

'On Sunday, then?'

She shook her head. 'It wouldn't be fair to keep presuming on your kindness.'

'Kindness be damned,' he exclaimed angrily. 'Annie, I think we could have the start of something wonderful here—'

'No, Gideon.'

'But, Annie, listen—'

She didn't. She simply swept a much-chastened Jamie out of the car and through the front door, and Gideon slammed his fist against his steering-wheel with frustration.

He could go after her, make her listen to him, but he knew it wouldn't do any good. Not right now, not when her emotions were far too raw.

But he could be patient, he decided as he sat in his car and waited until he saw the light come on in her living room. He could wait and be patient. If he backed off now, didn't hassle her, he might slowly but surely be able to break down the defensive wall she'd erected around herself.

He had to. For her sake and for his own, he had to.

CHAPTER SIX

'IT's nothing much—just a box of chocolates—but I really would like you to accept them as a thank-you present,' Carol Bannerman said, pressing the brightly wrapped box into Annie's surprised hands.

'But I haven't done anything,' Annie protested. 'Dr Brooke performed your fibroid operation.'

'I know, and I've already given him a bottle of wine, and I wanted to give one to Mr Caldwell, but Sister Baker said he doesn't usually get back from the operating theatre until half past two on Thursdays.'

Annie glanced down at her watch. 'It's only just gone half past.'

'Yes, but I'm afraid I can't wait any longer. Brian's arrived to take me home, you see, and he hates hospitals—can't abide them.' Carol dived into her overnight bag and produced a package. 'Would you give this to Mr Caldwell for me?'

Annie stared at the present uncomfortably. 'There's really no need for you to give us anything. I mean, it's very kind of you—and we appreciate the thought—but—'

'I *want* to do it, Doctor,' Carol declared. 'You see, when I saw you and Mr Caldwell I thought you were going to recommend a hysterectomy. My GP said you would. He said it was the best thing for my fibroids, but I knew if I had a hysterectomy…' She came to a halt, scrabbled for a handkerchief, then blew her nose noisily. 'Oh, cripes, I vowed I wouldn't do anything silly but the thing is, you've given me hope. Hope that I might still one day be able to have a baby, and a measly box of chocolates and two bottles of wine are small enough thanks for that.'

'I...I don't know what to say,' Annie faltered, immensely touched.

'Just don't tell me you're on a diet, and that Mr Caldwell and Dr Brooke are both teetotal,' Carol said with a shaky laugh, and Annie laughed, too.

'Have you an appointment for Mr Caldwell's outpatient clinic in a month's time?' she asked as she walked with Carol down the ward.

Carol nodded. 'He's lovely, isn't he—Mr Caldwell?'

'He's certainly an excellent consultant,' Annie replied noncommittally.

'I'm not talking about his qualifications,' Carol protested. 'I'm talking about *him*. OK, so maybe he's not drop-dead gorgeous, but there's something about him, don't you think?'

Too darned right there is, Annie thought, feeling her cheeks beginning to burn, and being a sensational kisser was just one of them.

'In fact, I can't understand why one of you hasn't snapped him up yet,' Carol continued. 'Frankly, I'd have been first in the queue myself if I didn't have Brian.'

I might have been right there with you after that kiss on Saturday, Annie thought as she waved Carol goodbye, if everything hadn't gone so horribly and terribly wrong.

Even now, almost a week later, she still couldn't sleep. The minute she drifted off, she began to dream. Dreams that were so vivid, so terrifying and real, that she had to rush immediately into Jamie's room to make sure he was still there, that she really had got him back.

David said she was overreacting.

He'd come round on Sunday morning, all agog to discover how her day out had gone. One look at her chalk-white face had been enough to make him deeply suspicious, but when Jamie had innocently announced that

Mummy had got very cross at the park, and they were never going there again, she'd been forced to tell him what had happened. It had been that, or allowing David to carry out his threat of going round to Gideon's flat to beat him to a pulp.

'Annie, it wasn't your fault, or Gideon's,' David said when she'd told him everything. 'So he kissed you. So you took your eyes off Jamie for a second—'

'It was a lot longer than a second,' she said, remembering, and her brother grinned.

'So he's a good kisser, is he?'

Good didn't come anywhere near to describing the effect of Gideon's lips on hers. That first touch of his mouth—so unbelievably sweet and tender—had been like coming home, like finding another part of her she hadn't even known was missing, but when he'd deepened the kiss… Lord, when he'd deepened the kiss she'd suddenly understood why romantic writers always wrote about bolts of lightning and soaring fireworks.

'Wow. That good, eh?' David laughed, watching her faraway expression, and Annie blushed and shook her head.

'It was a mistake, David. A mistake I won't let happen again.'

To her surprise, her brother actually looked angry.

'Annie, Jamie could have wandered off while you were out shopping, when you were in the post office, or in the bank. It's got nothing to do with you and Gideon kissing. And, yes, I know I wasn't sure about him at first,' he continued when she tried to protest, 'but I think he's a decent bloke, and it would be plain daft if you shut the door on something which could turn out to be pretty special because of some stupid guilt trip.'

Which was fine for him to say, Annie sighed, noticing that Rachel was beckoning to her, but David hadn't been there when Jamie had gone missing. He hadn't experienced those awful, terrifying, desperate minutes when she hadn't known where he was, and she never wanted to feel that way again. No matter what David said, it *had* been her fault. She should have been watching out for her son. She should have been concentrating on him, not kissing Gideon.

'Mrs Wilson says you've told her she might be able to get up for a little while today,' Woody said tightly.

'I said I would ask you or Dr Brooke if she could,' Annie said. 'She's getting so bored, you see,' she continued quickly, 'and I thought—'

'You are not here to think, Dr Hart, you are here to learn,' Woody snapped. 'And in future I'd be obliged if you left such important decisions to people who know considerably more than you do.'

A hot flush of colour washed over Annie's cheeks as the specialist registrar stalked away. Well, that was putting her in her place, and no mistake, and it wouldn't have been so bad if Kay hadn't heard every word.

'I'm really sorry, Doctor,' she said awkwardly. 'I didn't mean to get you into trouble.'

'You haven't,' Annie reassured her. Or at least no more in trouble with Woody than I normally am, she added mentally.

'She's really bossy, isn't she—Dr Dunwoody?' Kay continued. 'I mean, you, Mr Caldwell, Dr Brooke, Dr Fraser—you're all so kind and understanding—but Dr Dunwoody—'

'Have you had your blood pressure and temperature taken this afternoon?' Annie interrupted, knowing she had to put an end to this conversation, and fast. OK, so Woody wasn't exactly a little ray of sunshine, and she'd been more than usually snippy these past two weeks, but getting involved in a discussion about one of her superiors was a very bad idea.

'Sister Baker took them both about half an hour ago,' Kay replied. 'She said they were normal.'

'Well, that's good news, isn't it?' Annie said encouragingly, but Kay didn't look any happier.

'If my blood pressure and temperature are normal, why can't I get up? I'm fed up lying in this bed, staring at the same four walls. I want to go home.'

Annie sat down on the edge of the young woman's bed, and took her hand in hers. 'Kay, I know you're bored, but puerperal fever is a very dangerous disease and we want to make absolutely certain all the infection is gone before we discharge you.'

'Mr Caldwell said the same,' Kay declared belligerently, 'but I feel fine, Dr Hart—honestly I do—and I want to go home. I want to be a proper, normal mum, and see Gideon every day instead of just when he's brought into the ward for me to feed.'

'Gideon?' Annie repeated, her lips curving.

'My husband and I thought it would be nice to call the baby after Mr Caldwell.'

'Personally, I think it's a terrible idea,' a familiar deep voice commented. 'Why don't you call him something nice like Jack, or Scott, or Fraser?'

'Because we like Gideon, Mr Caldwell,' Kay said, beaming up at him. 'And Gideon is what he's going to be.'

'On your own heads be it, then,' Gideon said, his brown eyes twinkling. 'Everything OK here, Dr Hart?'

Should she ask him if Kay might get up for a little while? Bad idea, Annie, she told herself. Bypassing one of your superiors and going straight to the boss? Very, very bad idea indeed.

Kay, however, didn't suffer from any such inhibitions.

'Mr Caldwell, would it be all right if I got up for a little while?' she declared. 'I'm so bored, lying here all the time.'

He lifted the chart at the bottom of her bed. 'BP normal, temperature normal. OK, I don't see why not. No marathons, of course,' he added as Kay let out a whoop of delight. 'Just for half an hour today, and then we'll see about extending the time tomorrow if you don't suffer any after-effects.'

'Hallelujah!' Kay exclaimed. 'I was beginning to think I was rooted to this bed.'

'Well, we certainly can't have that.' He grinned, and, with a smile and a nod at Annie, walked away.

Which was exactly what she wanted, she told herself, determinedly refusing to allow her eyes to follow him. The occasional smile, the once-in-a-while pleasantry and conversations which were friendly without being over-friendly.

It was what she'd got, too. Ever since Monday morning when she'd crept unwillingly into work, wondering if she might have to resign if working with him should prove impossible, he'd been the perfect gentleman. Pleasant, courteous, unfailingly polite—and it was annoying the hell out of her.

Which was crazy.

Good heavens, it wasn't as though she *wanted* him collaring her in corners, attempting to argue her out of her decision, so she ought to be pleased that he'd accepted her decision without question, and she was, but…

'You're looking a bit glum, Annie,' Helen observed when they met halfway down the ward. 'Anything wrong?'

'I'm just a bit tired today, that's all,' Annie replied, forcing a smile to her lips.

'Gideon was down in the doldrums, too, a couple of weeks ago,' the SHO observed, 'but he seems a lot more upbeat nowadays. Happier, and more positive somehow, if you know what I mean.'

Annie did, and that was bugging her as well. OK, so

she hadn't wanted to see him moping around the ward, or chewing everybody's head off because she wouldn't go out with him again, but neither had she expected him to be so apparently unaffected by her rebuff. Their kiss had been mind-blowing on anybody's scale of kisses, and at least she'd thought he might have made *some* token effort to overcome her scruples.

Not that she'd have given in to any of his arguments, of course, she told herself severely, but still…

'Did you and Gideon have a nice day out at the Botanic Gardens last Saturday?'

Annie almost tripped over the drugs trolley. 'How did you…?'

'One of my friends was there with her kids.' Helen smiled. 'She knows Gideon, and from the description she gave me of the girl he was with, I'm guessing it was you.'

'Yes, it was me,' Annie muttered.

'My friend said you and your son seemed to be really enjoying yourselves.'

Helen's eyes were fixed on her with keen interest, and Annie's jaw set. She knew exactly what the SHO was up to. Before—when Helen had made all those weird, veiled comments about Gideon being such a decent bloke, and how he needed somebody in his life—she'd been completely bewildered, but now she wasn't. Now she very strongly suspected that Helen was trying to set her up with their boss. She could forget it.

'We had a very pleasant day out, but we've no plans to repeat it,' she said firmly.

'Not yet, you mean.' Helen smiled.

'Not ever,' Annie declared even more firmly, but to her acute annoyance the SHO's smile merely widened. 'Now look, Helen—'

'Sorry, to interrupt, Doctors,' Liz said, 'but Louise Harper's just about ready to leave, and I understand from

Gideon that Annie's going to speak to her before she goes.'

'I am?' Annie said faintly, hoping against hope that she might have misheard, but knowing she hadn't.

'Apparently he wants you to make certain she understands the importance of taking her medication,' Liz continued, 'and of attending his clinic in a month's time.'

Then why can't he do it? Annie thought, reluctantly forcing her feet out of the ward and along to Room 3. Or Helen, or Woody, or Tom? Why does it have to be me, when talks with Louise always leave me feeling so depressed and disheartened?

Because it's part of your job, she told herself severely. Every patient can't leave the ward laughing. Some of them are going to be upset, or frightened, or tearful.

Louise looked to be all three, Annie thought with a sinking heart when she put her head tentatively round the girl's door.

'All set to go, then, Louise?' she asked with determined brightness.

'I guess so,' the girl muttered.

'Have you got the antibiotics Mr Caldwell prescribed for you?'

Louise held up her handbag. 'They're in here. And, yes, I know I have to complete the whole course,' she said when Annie opened her mouth to say just that. 'Even if I feel OK, I've got to take every pill.'

Annie smiled. 'Just so long as you don't forget. Has Sister Baker made an appointment for you at Mr Caldwell's outpatient clinic?'

'Yes. I've got my appointment card.'

Lord, but she looked so very young, Annie thought as she gazed at the girl's lowered head. OK, so she wasn't old—just gone eighteen—but this morning she looked even younger. Young, and alone, and totally defeated.

'Louise—'

'I'd better get going,' the girl interrupted. 'Sister Baker has called me a taxi, and I don't want to keep it waiting—not with what taxis charge nowadays.'

'Do you have somewhere to stay?' Annie asked as the girl began putting on her coat. 'I know you used to live with your boyfriend—'

'A friend is going to put me up for a couple of weeks until I find somewhere else.'

It sounded a singularly miserable homecoming to Annie, and she cleared her throat hesitantly. 'I take it there's no chance… I mean, your boyfriend…?'

'He wouldn't come near me now with a ten-foot barge-pole,' Louise said bitterly. 'You heard what he said when he visited me.'

Annie had. So had the entire ward.

'He was frightened, Louise, upset—'

'So that's why he called me a slag and a whore, is it?'

Annie winced. It had been a horrible episode. Louise's boyfriend had arrived, bearing a huge bunch of flowers, but the minute she'd told him what was wrong, and that he might need treatment himself, he'd exploded. He called Louise every insulting name under the sun, vehemently denying that there was anything wrong with him, and he'd still been screaming abuse when Gideon had forcibly ejected him.

'Louise, why don't I phone your mother?' Annie said quickly. 'I know you didn't want her to know you were in hospital, but—'

'And have her say "I told you so"?' Louise shook her head. 'She always used to say I'd come to a bad end, and it looks like she was right.'

'Oh, Louise, you haven't come to a bad end,' Annie protested. 'OK, so you've had pelvic inflammatory disease—'

'Mr Caldwell said I'll never conceive a baby naturally,' Louise said, tears welling in her eyes. 'He said I'll have to have IVF treatment if I want one, but one of my cousins has been on an IVF waiting list for years. She and her husband have been waiting for treatment for *years*.'

'I'm sure by the time you want to have a baby things will be better—quicker,' Annie said, desperately trying to remain upbeat. 'Look, Louise, I know it seems like the end of the world right now—'

'It *is* the end of the world,' the girl cried. 'What decent man is going to come anywhere near me, Doctor? What decent bloke is going to want to have anything to do with a girl who's had a sexually transmitted disease?'

Tears were rolling down Louise's cheeks now, running into her nose and mouth, and Annie put her arms round her quickly. 'Louise, it wasn't your fault you got PID. And as for finding a decent man, there's thousands of men out there.'

'That's what Mr Caldwell said,' the girl sobbed. 'He said all men weren't low-life stinkers.'

'Then believe him,' Annie insisted. 'Believe him, and start looking forward, not back. I wish we could erase what's happened to you, but we can't. It's happened, and it's awful, but it's over. Look forward now, not back.'

And I'm the biggest hypocrite of all time, she thought as Louise sobbed into her shoulder. For the past four years everything I've done—every thought and action—has been governed by my past. I won't get involved with a man because I'm frightened he'll hurt me as Nick did. I've knocked back a perfectly decent bloke like Gideon Caldwell because I'm frightened he'll hurt me, too.

I've got to start looking forward, too, and not back. I've got to let go of my past, but I don't know if I can. I truly, honestly, don't know if I can.

It took her more than an hour to calm Louise down sufficiently for her to be able to leave, and by then all Annie wanted was some peace and quiet, and a cup of coffee in the staffroom. The coffee was certainly there, but peace was quite clearly not on the agenda. Not judging by the gleaming light in Liz's eyes.

'You are *never* going to believe what I've got to tell you,' she said the minute she saw Annie.

'Woody's been kidnapped by white-slave traffickers, and they're refusing to give her back,' Annie replied, reaching for the coffee-jar.

'It's almost as unlikely, but nope. Try again.'

Annie shook her head. 'Liz, I'm not in the mood for guessing games. Can't you simply tell me?'

'You're no fun, you know that?'

'Liz.'

'Oh, all right, then. Gideon—our Gideon—is going to the St Valentine's Ball tomorrow night.'

'That's hardly earth-shattering news,' Annie protested. 'You said he always attends hospital functions, buys screeds of raffle tickets, dances with the consultants' wives…'

'Yes, but he's just bought *two* tickets from me.'

'Two?' Annie faltered.

'That's what I thought.' Liz nodded, unwrapping a chocolate bar and taking a large bite. 'He's obviously got a date for tomorrow. Talk about still waters and dark horses. I wonder who she is?'

Annie wondered, too. It certainly wasn't her. Not that she'd have gone to the ball with him if he'd asked, of course, but he hadn't asked.

'I wonder if it's that busty new nurse in Paediatrics,' Liz continued thoughtfully. 'The blonde one with the dark roots. She's been after him since the day she arrived.'

'She has?'

'Oh, Annie, don't you notice *anything*?' Liz protested. 'Good grief, the woman's been up and down to this ward practically every day for the last three weeks, and it's not been to see me, that's for sure.'

Annie frowned. She had a vague memory of seeing a

blonde nurse flitting about the place, but she hadn't paid any attention. She wished she had now. She wished even more that she wasn't experiencing something which felt disturbingly like jealousy.

'Maybe he's taking Helen,' she suggested. 'She wanted to go to the ball, remember, but Tom wanted to watch that football match.'

'Oh, Helen put the kibosh on that plan ages ago,' Liz declared. 'They're coming to the ball together. Nope, Gideon's definitely got a date, and I wish I knew who it was. I hope it's not that frosty-faced new receptionist in Radiology. She wouldn't suit Gideon at all.'

'I wasn't aware he was such a popular man,' Annie said more tartly than she'd intended, and Liz chuckled.

'Oh, you wouldn't believe how many women have made a play for our Gideon. Normally it seems to go right over his head, but somebody must have grabbed his interest or he wouldn't have bought two tickets for the ball, would he?'

Annie was saved from answering by the staffroom phone, and by the time Liz had put it down one look at her grim face was enough to banish all thoughts of Gideon and the Valentine's Ball from her mind.

'What is it—what's happened?' she asked, as Liz threw the remnants of her chocolate biscuit into the bin.

'Jennifer Norton's on her way in. She's bleeding.'

'She's Gideon's IVF patient, isn't she?' Annie queried. 'The one who's on her fourth IVF treatment?'

Liz nodded. 'I really thought she was going to make it this time, but she's just eight weeks so…' She sighed. 'Could you page Gideon for me while I get hold of the ultrasound technician?'

Annie didn't need to. The door of the staffroom suddenly swung open and Gideon appeared.

'Liz, those reports you gave me to sign. You said there were thirty of them, but I've only got—'

'Forget the reports,' she interrupted. 'Jennifer Norton's coming in. Vaginal bleeding.'

He swore under his breath. 'Have you organised an ultrasound?'

'Just doing it,' Liz replied, swiftly dialling the number.

'It might not be a miscarriage,' Annie said, seeing the deep frown on Gideon's face. 'Just because she's bleeding doesn't necessarily mean—' She came to a halt as the lift pinged. 'Is that her?'

He nodded grimly. 'Could you come with me, Annie? I may need your help.'

Quickly she followed him into the corridor, and her heart went out to the woman who was being wheeled towards them. It was obvious that Jennifer and her husband were convinced she'd had a miscarriage. She was sitting hunched in a wheelchair, sobbing uncontrollably, while her husband walked beside her, white-lipped and grim.

'I wasn't doing anything I shouldn't, Mr Caldwell, honestly I wasn't,' Jennifer exclaimed as soon as she saw him. 'I just bent down to get a pot out of the cupboard, and then I felt such a pain, and—'

'I told her I would do all the cooking,' her husband interrupted defensively. 'I told her to leave everything to me, to take things easy.'

'Lifting a pot wouldn't have brought on a miscarriage,' Gideon said soothingly, while the porter wheeled Jennifer into one of their private rooms. 'And we don't even know if she's actually had a miscarriage yet. Many women have some spotting right up until twenty-five weeks.'

'But it was such a lot of blood, Mr Caldwell,' Jennifer wept. 'It wasn't just a little bit. There was so much of it which means I've definitely lost the baby, and I can't bear it. I *can't*.'

'Jennifer, we're not going to know anything until we've done a scan,' Gideon said as the ultrasound technician arrived. 'So until we know something I want you to try to relax. I know that's asking a lot,' he continued when another sob broke from her, 'but the calmer you are, the better the pictures will be. Annie, could you…?'

She nodded and gently eased Jennifer's loose-fitting trousers down to smooth the conductive jelly onto her abdomen.

Once that was done there was nothing else they could do but wait. Wait while the technician swept the probe over Jennifer's stomach. Wait until the monitor revealed whether the tiny embryo was still there or not.

Gideon's eyes were fixed on the screen, searching, searching, but as Annie watched him, hoping to see from his expression whether it was good news or bad, she suddenly noticed something else. His hands were clenched into tight, hard fists by his sides.

He really cared about this baby. Not because he was the consultant who had carried out the IVF treatment and wanted it to succeed to demonstrate his skill. He cared because it was a new life, and infinitely precious to Jennifer and her husband.

This man wasn't Nick, who'd taken, and taken, and never given. He wasn't Nick, who'd never done anything, or said anything, without an ulterior motive. He was honest and genuine, and yet she'd told him she never wanted to go out with him again.

Annie must have made some small inarticulate sound because Gideon's eyes suddenly flicked towards her, and he smiled. A smile of such heart-stopping warmth that tears filled her eyes. The baby was all right—that much was clear—but what was even clearer to her was how much of a fool she was.

'Could you print out a still for me, please?' Gideon asked the technician, then turned to Jennifer. 'I want you to take a look at this, Jennifer,' he continued, pointing at the monitor. 'Do you see those two fluttering movements—like tiny butterfly wings? Those are your babies' heartbeats.'

'Babies?' Mr Norton echoed, looking stunned. 'But surely there should only be one. Jennifer—she was bleeding and—'

'If you remember, we put three embryos back into your wife in an attempt to maximise the chances of success,' Gideon explained. 'Generally only one implants properly and goes on to become a baby, but in Jennifer's case it looks as though two have.'

'And the bleeding?'

'I don't know what caused it,' Gideon admitted. 'It could be the third embryo has just failed, or—'

'Are you saying the other babies might fail, too?' Jennifer interrupted, panic appearing on her face.

'I don't know, Jennifer,' he said gently. 'All I can say is that at the moment you're still pregnant with twins, so hold onto that, OK?'

The technician had printed out a black and white photograph showing the grainy outline of the two babies. As Jennifer and her husband gazed at it in wonder, Liz appeared in the doorway.

'Do you want her to stay in, Gideon?' she murmured. 'I've managed to find her a bed but if you don't need it…'

'I think she'd better stay,' he answered, keeping his voice as low as hers. 'She's had one hell of a fright—given me one, too—and though there's nothing we can actually do if she does start to lose the other babies, it might keep her calmer if she stays with us for a couple of days.'

Liz nodded, and within minutes Jennifer was being whisked into one of the beds on the ward. Annie and Gideon stayed with her until she was settled, and eventually Jennifer fell asleep, clearly worn out by the events of the day.

Gideon looked exhausted, too, and Annie shook her head at him as she accompanied him out of the ward.

'When was the last time you left the hospital early—got ten hours' unbroken sleep?'

He smiled a little ruefully. 'I haven't a clue. The trouble is we really need another doctor on the team, and I've been trying to get Admin to agree to it, but...' He shrugged. 'I don't mind the extra work—not really. It's not as though I've got somebody to rush home to.'

Tell him, Annie, her heart whispered. Tell him you've changed your mind, that you'd very much like to go out with him again.

'Gideon—'

'You'd better start heading for home,' he commented. 'It must be well past four o'clock.'

It was, and the staff at the day-care centre were going to raise merry hell again, but she knew that if she didn't say what she wanted to now she never would.

'Gideon—'

'Could I have a word with you, please, Gideon?' Rachel interrupted, appearing beside them without warning. 'In private,' she added, her gaze irritably sweeping over Annie.

He nodded. 'If you'd like to go along to my consulting room, I'll be with you in a minute.' The specialist registrar stalked away, and he sighed. 'No rest for the wicked.'

'No,' Annie murmured, but he didn't move and neither did she.

'How's Jamie?' he asked.

'Full of beans as usual.' She fiddled with the buttons on her white coat. 'He...he asked me to thank you for taking him to the Botanic Gardens. He really enjoyed himself.'

'So did I.'

His voice was soft, gentle, and she bit her lip.

Say it, Annie, she told herself. Good grief, how hard

can it be to tell him you want to go out with him again? It's not like you're suggesting moving in with him. Only to get to know him better. To take it slowly, one step at a time.

But what if he's not interested any more? a warning voice pointed out. He's not tried to talk you out of the decision you made on Saturday, and he's got a date for tomorrow night. A date for the St Valentine's Ball with the busty new nurse in Paediatrics or the frosty-faced new receptionist in Radiology. You're going to look really stupid if you tell him you've changed your mind, only to discover he has as well.

'Annie…?'

Gideon was waiting, clearly becoming more and more perplexed by the second, and she backed up a step.

'You're right—I'd better go,' she said, and turned round and walked away.

Coward, her heart mocked when she reached the staff-room. Coward. Chicken.

Better a chicken than an idiot, she thought, but was it?

Nobody had ever died of embarrassment. They might feel as though they'd like to, but they never had. Two minutes was all it would take to go to his room and tell him, and those two minutes might lead to the start of something wonderful.

Do it, Annie, her heart urged, and before she'd even realised she was moving she was hurrying back down the corridor towards his room.

'I've changed my mind, Gideon,' she muttered out loud as she walked along. 'That's all I have to say. No big preamble, no lengthy explanation, just, "If it's not too late, Gideon, I've changed my mind."'

She could do it—she knew she could—but she didn't get the chance to.

The door of Gideon's room was open. Nothing unusual

about that, of course. He often didn't close it so that anyone passing could drop in for a chat, but he wasn't alone.

Woody was with him.

Woody was standing wrapped in Gideon's arms. Her head was resting on his shoulder, and when Annie saw him bend his head to kiss her she turned on her heel and ran.

CHAPTER SEVEN

'I LIKE Gideon.' Jamie scraped the last remnants of his breakfast cereal from his plate and put down his spoon. 'Why don't we see him any more?'

'You've hardly seen him a lot, Jamie,' Annie protested. 'In fact, you've only seen him once.'

'Two times, Mummy. Once when he came round to our house, and the other time when he took us to the park. I liked the park. Could we go there again with Gideon? I won't wander off this time—I promise I won't. Can we go to the park with Gideon again?'

'He's a very busy man, sweetheart.'

'He said we could go,' Jamie protested. 'When we had our hamburgers and chips he said he'd like to go back. We could go tomorrow—'

'I'm working tomorrow.'

'On Sunday, then. We could go on Sunday.'

'Look, why don't I ask your Uncle David to take us?' Annie said desperately. 'We could go in his big red Volvo—'

'Uncle David doesn't like the park as much as Gideon does. Gideon really, *really* likes the park. If we went there with him we could feed the squirrels this time and look at the big goldfish again. Gideon liked the goldfish. He said—'

'Jamie, will you stop wittering on about the damn park?' Annie snapped, then bit her lip when her son's lip began to tremble. 'I'm sorry, sweetheart. Mummy... Mummy has a bit of a headache this morning.'

A headache which had started yesterday. A headache which had begun the second she'd flown out of the hos-

116

pital, running as though all the devils in hell had been after her.

Rachel Dunwoody.

How in the world could Gideon be attracted to somebody like Rachel Dunwoody? If it had been anybody else...

Liar, her heart jeered. You'd have cared no matter who it had been because you're half in love with him. Half in love with a man you've only been out with once. Half in love with a man whose kiss was like nothing you've ever experienced before, and now you're angry, and confused, and jealous.

Too damn right I'm angry, she thought as she carried Jamie's cereal bowl across to the sink. Trust me, he'd said. I'll never hurt you, he'd said. And yet last night his arms had been around Woody. He'd been kissing Woody.

'Mummy, is Gideon my daddy?'

The cereal bowl slipped from Annie's fingers and landed in the sink with a clatter. Where in the world had that come from? Jamie had never asked about his father before. She'd known he would eventually, but why now, and why had he decided Gideon must be the man?

'No, he's not,' she said as calmly as she could. 'He's my boss.'

'Ben at the centre has a daddy,' Jamie continued, his small forehead creased in thought. 'Josh has a daddy. Emma Harding has *two*. One for week times and one for the weekend. Why don't I have a daddy?'

'You do,' Annie said awkwardly. 'He just...he doesn't live with us.'

Jamie's frown deepened. 'I'd like Gideon to be my daddy. He knows all about trees and squirrels, and he could take us to the park every weekend, and—'

'Jamie, Gideon is not going to be your daddy,' she said firmly. 'So can we just drop the subject, please?'

Her son stared at her for a moment, then got down from his seat. 'Well, I like him,' he muttered.

So do I, Annie thought with a sharp twist of pain. In fact, I was beginning to think… Unconsciously she shook her head. It didn't matter what she thought any more.

Wearily she ran some water into the sink, then saw the time. 'We've got to go, Jamie, or we'll be late.'

'Don't care.'

'Well, I do,' she said, taking his coat down from the back of the door. 'I'm assisting Dr Brooke in the operating theatre this morning.'

'Don't care,' he repeated, even more belligerently. 'Want to stay home. Want you to stay home, too.'

Not that again. Not this morning when she already felt strung out and exhausted and her day hadn't even begun.

'I don't care what you want,' she said, catching hold of his hand and forcing him into his coat. 'You are going to the centre, and you are going now.'

He howled the whole way. People stared, people shook their heads, and Annie didn't know what she felt most— mortification, anger or guilt.

'He'll be fine, Dr Hart,' the assistant at the day-care centre declared when she arrived. 'Once he's met all his little friends, started to play with them, he'll be fine.'

He probably would, she thought as she trudged wearily to the hospital. Children's memories were notoriously short. She wished hers was. She wished even more that she hadn't gone to Gideon's room last night.

Still waters and dark horses, Liz had said. Well, they certainly didn't get much deeper or darker than Gideon Caldwell. Kissing her on Saturday, Rachel Dunwoody on Thursday, and goodness knows how many other women in between.

How could she have been so wrong about him? He'd seemed so genuine—so honest and different—but when it came right down to it, he was no better than Nick.

Helen obviously didn't agree with her. In fact, Helen was bubbling with delight when they met outside the staffroom.

'A little bird's just told me you're going to the ball tonight with Gideon.' She beamed. 'Oh, Annie, I couldn't be more pleased—'

'Or more wrong,' Annie interrupted. 'I don't know who told you that.'

'Liz did. Well, to be fair, she didn't exactly say you were going with Gideon,' Helen conceded, 'but when she told me he'd bought two tickets—'

'Helen, I am not—repeat *not*—going anywhere with Gideon Caldwell. Not tonight—not any night.'

'You're not?' the SHO said, her delight giving way to a puzzled frown. 'Then who's he going with?'

Annie could have told her. She could also have said that far from appearing to have difficulty in talking to women on a personal level, Gideon was, in fact, a world expert, but she didn't.

'I haven't the faintest idea,' she said instead. 'And now, if you'll excuse me, I'm assisting Tom in Theatre this morning.'

At least that's what the roster had said she'd be doing, but when she reached Theatre 2 it wasn't Tom who turned to smile at her. It was Gideon. Gideon all dressed up in theatre scrubs and ready to go.

'I thought— I mean, isn't Tom scheduled to operate this morning?' she said with barely concealed dismay.

'There's been a change of plan,' Gideon said, 'so I'm afraid you're stuck with me.'

'Stuck' being the operative word, Annie thought crossly as she pulled a set of theatre scrubs from the cupboard. What was the point of having schedules if nobody kept to them? She'd been looking forward to some hopefully peaceful hours of instructive surgery with Tom, and who had she got instead? The Belfield's answer to Casanova.

'Is something wrong?' Gideon continued, his smile fading as she stalked past him towards one of the changing cubicles. 'You're looking a bit flushed.'

'I'm fine,' she replied, her voice tight, cold.

'You're sure?' he pressed. 'Because if you're not feeling well I could page Helen, get her to assist—'

'I said I'm fine,' she snapped, slamming the cubicle door on him, only to lean against it with a groan.

Brilliant, Annie, really brilliant. How is biting the man's head off going to solve anything? He's your boss, for heaven's sake, and who he kisses is none of your damn business. You're not his girlfriend. You and Jamie have been out with him precisely once. You've no claim on him—no right to be angry. It was one measly kiss, that's all, so unless you're planning on looking for another job, back off, simmer down and be polite.

But I don't want to be polite, her heart protested. I want to pummel him senseless. I want to kick his shins, and demand to know what the hell he thinks he's playing at. And then—and this is the really, *really* crazy part—I want to howl my eyes out.

Unfortunately, none of those options were starters if she wanted to hold onto her job, and reluctantly she put on her theatre scrubs, and even more reluctantly opened the changing-room door to find Gideon still standing where she'd left him.

'I…I'm sorry,' she forced herself to say. 'I shouldn't have snapped at you, but I…I didn't sleep very well last night.'

'There's no need to apologise,' he said gently. 'As long as you're OK, that's all that matters.'

But I'm not OK, she thought, edging past him to the sink. I'm angry and disappointed, and the last thing I want from you is kindness. Not when you obviously don't mean it. Not when you probably said exactly the same thing to Woody last night.

'How's Jamie?' he asked, when they began scrubbing up.

Like she was supposed to think he cared? 'Fine,' she replied.

'No more trouble getting him to the day-care centre?'

Don't do this to me, her heart cried. Don't pretend to be interested in me and my son when I know you're not. Don't stand there looking all nice, and dependable, and downright attractive, because I can't handle it.

'He's fine,' she repeated.

'And David?' he said, stretching across her to get more soap just as she did, too.

Their collision was inevitable. While her hands went up instinctively to prevent it, she still ended up nose first in his chest. Nose first into a chest that smelt of hospital antiseptic, pine soap and something else that was simply him. Nose first into a pair of arms with dark hairs that brushed against her own bare arms as they reached out to steady her, sending tantalising shivers racing up and down her spine.

She should have stepped back immediately, of course. Any sensible woman would have stepped back immediately, but all her sense seemed to have gone west in the confines of his arms.

'Annie…'

His voice was deep, husky against her ear, and she raised her head slowly. It was her second mistake. The moment she gazed into his deep brown eyes she was lost. She didn't even try to evade his lips when they lowered to capture hers. In fact, she angled her head for him. Slid her arms up his back to hold him closer, and groaned as he plundered her mouth with his tongue, teasing and encouraging her to respond with a fervour she hadn't even known she'd possessed.

It was only when she suddenly became aware of the hard evidence of his arousal through the thin material of their theatre scrubs that reality struck home. Struck home with all the force of a cold shower. With a strangled cry she pulled herself free from his arms.

'Annie, it's all right,' he said, his breathing fast and ragged as she backed away from him, shaking her head from side to side.

But it wasn't all right, she thought as she stared up at him. How could she have been so weak, so *stupid*? Last night this man had been making love to Woody, and she—idiot that she was—had just fallen into his arms as well.

'Annie—'

'We…we'll have to scrub up again,' she said, spinning back to the sink, her cheeks scarlet with angry, mortified colour.

'But, Annie—'

'Gideon, what happened… I blame myself.'

'There's no question of blame,' he protested. 'Annie, we're both grown-up, single, unattached.'

You're not, she wanted to hurl back at him, but didn't. 'We have patients waiting, Gideon.'

For a moment she thought he was going to argue with her, then he nodded slowly. 'OK, but we need to talk about this, Annie. Later we really have got to talk.'

Not in my lifetime, she thought as she squeezed more soap onto her hands and saw they were shaking. She knew what would happen if they talked. He would look at her with those tender, concerned brown eyes of his, and all her common sense would disappear straight out the window.

Well, not any more, she told herself firmly when they reached the operating theatre and she watched him perform Mrs Burns's tubal occlusion and Mrs Simpson's hysterectomy. He was the still waters and dark horse man with a nice line in sympathetic smiles and understanding looks, but it was just that—a line—and she wasn't buying. Not now. Not ever.

'Last patient coming up,' Gideon declared when he'd completed Mrs Simpson's hysterectomy. 'It's Sylvia Renton. I know she's only thirty-two weeks, but I've decided to perform a Caesarean. She's getting no better psychologically, and I don't think it's good for either her or the child to postpone the delivery any longer.'

Annie nodded. Over the past week she'd noticed Sylvia was becoming more and more antagonistic towards the child she was carrying, and the woman's attitude didn't appear to have changed when she was wheeled into the operating theatre, her white-faced, be-gowned husband at her side.

'I don't care what you do,' she told Gideon when he'd explained about the epidural anaesthetic which would ensure she wouldn't feel any pain and yet would allow her to see her baby the second it was born. 'Just so long as you get rid of this sickness.'

'We can certainly guarantee that.' He smiled. 'And I'm sure that once you see your son or daughter you'll feel it's all been worthwhile.'

Sylvia didn't look convinced. Annie wasn't either when the intensive care baby unit team took up their positions, a humidicrib at the ready. Sylvia's pregnancy had been so unrelentingly miserable that to expect her to immediately bond with her baby was expecting a lot, but miracles did happen.

'Everyone ready?' Gideon asked once he'd injected the anaesthetic into Sylvia's spine and Annie had inserted a catheter into her bladder to drain it.

They all nodded. Even Pete Renton from where he was standing nervously positioned behind the green screen which they'd erected over his wife's torso so that he wouldn't see the actual operation but would be able to get his first glimpse of his child.

With ample blood supplies at the ready in case Sylvia should unexpectedly require a transfusion, Gideon swiftly made a horizontal incision into her stomach just above her pubic bone, and then another down into her uterus. Gently he freed the baby's head and while one of the theatre nurses suctioned off the amniotic fluid Annie pressed down on the top of Sylvia's womb so that Gideon could lift the baby out.

'It's a boy, love,' Mr Renton declared excitedly. 'At least…' He frowned. 'At least I think it is.'

'It is, indeed.' Gideon chuckled, handing the baby to a member of the intensive care baby unit once he'd clipped and cut the cord.

Lord, but he was so small, Annie thought, tears welling in her eyes as the nurse showed Sylvia and her husband their son before placing it in the humidicrib. He weighed scarcely more than a bag of flour, but at least he'd taken his first breath. She'd heard it—a tiny wail like that of a kitten—and she'd seen his little fists move before the ICBU team had whisked him away.

'Annie.'

Her head snapped round guiltily. 'I…I'm sorry, I—'

'He'll be fine,' Gideon said, understanding in his voice. 'He may be small, but he's perfectly formed. The most important thing now is to make sure we've removed all the afterbirth from mum.'

She flushed under her mask. He must think her a complete idiot, being on the verge of tears when she was supposed to be assisting him. But Sylvia had scarcely looked at her son, and she couldn't help but remember the day Jamie was born. The almost terrifying rush of love she'd felt when she'd stared down at him and realised he was part of her, her own flesh and blood.

'I'm just going to give you another injection, Sylvia,' Gideon said. 'It's a drug called ergometrine, which will make your uterus contract and stop any bleeding. Once that's taken effect, and we've stitched you up again, one of the staff from the intensive care baby unit will wheel you along to see your son.'

'I'd far rather get some sleep,' she replied, and Gideon's eyes met Annie's across the operating table.

'I'm sure you would,' she said smoothly. 'But I'm equally certain that you'll sleep a lot easier after you've seen your son again.'

'He's beautiful, love,' Pete enthused. 'In fact, he looks just like you.'

'Does he,' Sylvia said without interest.

'And he's got such a head of hair—really thick, and long,' her husband continued. 'Sylvia, he's gorgeous.'

'I'm just glad he's not making me sick any more,' she muttered.

'We'll give her a couple of days to recover from the op,' Gideon commented once he and Annie were back in the changing room, 'but if her attitude towards the baby doesn't improve I'll ask the hospital psychiatrist to have a word.'

'At least Mr Renton was pleased,' she said, pulling off her cap and binning it.

'Sylvia will be eventually,' he said. 'I've seen situations like this before, and the secret is to do something about it quickly before it festers and becomes a big problem.'

'I guess so,' she said without conviction.

'You did very well this morning,' he continued. 'Woody told me you have good hands, and you do.'

He'd meant it as a compliment, but Annie didn't appear to take it as such. In fact, to his amazement, she shot him a look which would have sunk a lesser mortal.

Now, what on earth was that all about? he wondered as she went abruptly into the changing room. OK, so perhaps she was still upset about their kiss earlier, but the look she'd given him hadn't been an unhappy one. It had been positively venomous.

She obviously thought their kiss had been a big mistake, but what the hell had he been supposed to do? She'd looked so damned desirable, her cheeks all flushed, her eyes softly luminous, and backing off as he'd been doing for the past week, not crowding or hassling her, sure as heck hadn't worked. If anything, he thought she'd become even more uptight and tense in his presence.

He pulled off his theatre top with a sigh. It looked like it was time for plan B. Plan A definitely hadn't worked so it was time for plan B. He just hoped he could pull it off.

'A staff meeting!' Helen exclaimed belligerently. 'Why the heck does Gideon want to hold a staff meeting today of all days? I was hoping to get away on time. I've got an appointment at the hairdresser's for the ball tonight, then I've got to dash home and get the kids fed and settled before the babysitter arrives—'

'What's the meeting about?' Annie interrupted.

'I haven't a clue. Three o'clock prompt in his room—that's all he said.' The SHO's gaze raked over Annie. 'You look terrible. You're not coming down with something, are you?'

I wish I was, Annie thought ruefully. If I was coming down with something there'd be some medicine I could take, some pill that would make me feel better, but there isn't a pill to cure anger and disappointment.

'I'm fine,' she said, suddenly realising Helen was waiting for a reply.

'You're sure? Only you're looking very peaky, and—Oh, damn,' Helen groaned as her bleeper went off. 'Why do I just know it's going to be one of those days?'

'Tell me about it,' Annie sighed when Helen hurried off. At least the SHO had something to look forward to tonight. At least she was secure in her husband's love, even if he didn't always remember to send her a card on Valentine's Day.

Actually, none of the women on the ward appeared to have been forgotten. Every bed had flowers or a card beside it. Some even had heart-shaped balloons to commemorate the day, and what had she got? Nothing. A big fat nothing.

No, not nothing, she thought as she noticed Jennifer Norton flicking through a magazine, then throwing it aside. You've got your son, and he's the most precious, wonderful thing in your life.

'How are you feeling, Jennifer?' she asked, pulling up a chair beside the woman's bed.

'OK, I guess,' Jennifer began, then shook her head. 'No, I'm not. I'm terrified. Terrified to move. Terrified even to turn over in case...'

'Jennifer, if your two remaining embryos are securely implanted, you'd have to go horse riding to dislodge them, and you probably wouldn't even be able to do it then,' Annie told her.

'That's what Mr Caldwell said, but he's talking about sending me home on Monday or Tuesday, and I don't want to go home,' Jennifer said, obviously perilously close to tears. 'I want to stay here for the whole of my pregnancy, and then I know everything will be all right.'

'Oh, Jennifer—'

'Don't tell me my favourite mum-to-be is getting herself down in the dumps again?'

Was Gideon haunting her today? Annie thought with irritation, turning to see him standing behind her. No, of course he wasn't. He was simply doing his afternoon rounds, but it *felt* like he was haunting her.

'Couldn't we possibly keep her in a little longer?' she asked as she followed him down the ward after he'd done his best to reassure Jennifer. 'Perhaps for a week—ten days?'

'Annie, it isn't going to make any difference if Jennifer's here or at home, and much as I'd like to sit by her bed, holding her hand for the duration of her pregnancy, we don't have the spare bed capacity.'

He was right, they didn't.

'I just hope she makes it,' she murmured, glancing over her shoulder in time to see Jennifer pick up her magazine again.

'So do I, but one thing I've learned from my years of medicine is that hopes aren't always realised.' He glanced down at his watch. 'It's almost three o'clock. I'll try my best to keep this staff meeting as short as possible so you can get away in time to pick up Jamie.'

Gideon was doing it again—being kind, thoughtful—and before she could stop herself she said tartly, 'I don't want—or need—any favours from you.'

He blinked. 'I'm sorry?'

'Not half as sorry as I am,' she muttered under her breath, but he must have heard her because as she swung out of the ward he hurried after her and caught hold of her arm.

'Look, what is this?' he demanded, spinning her round to face him. 'You've been shooting daggers at me all day, and if I'm in the doghouse I'd at least like to know the reason.'

'If you don't know, I'm certainly not going to tell you,' she retorted, which was silly and childish, but right now she didn't feel very grown up.

He let go of her arm and wearily dragged his fingers through his hair making it even more unruly than normal. 'Annie, it's been a rough week, and I have every expectation that next week's going to be even rougher. If this is all because I kissed you, I'm not going to apologise. I enjoyed it, and I think you did, too.'

'I'm surprised you can even remember it!' she exclaimed. 'One kiss amongst so many.'

'So many?' he repeated in apparent confusion, then sighed. 'Annie, it's been a long day, and I'm tired. Just tell me what's bugging you, OK?'

She opened her mouth, then closed it again. Like she could simply say that she'd seen him kissing Rachel Dunwoody last night, and she thought he was a rat? No, she didn't think so.

'Your private life is none of my business,' she said instead.

'What private life?' he protested. 'I come to work—I work—then I go home again. Jeez, Annie, anyone would think you were suggesting I was the Belfield's answer to Casanova.'

'From what I've heard and seen, you are.'

The accusation was out before she could stop it, and his jaw dropped. 'I beg your pardon?'

'So you should,' she retorted, the anger she'd been feeling all day suddenly bubbling over. 'Trust me, you said. I'll never hurt you, you said. And the stupid thing is, I was beginning to believe you.'

He stared at her silently for a second, then shook his head. 'My father warned me that women could be irrational, and now I see why. OK, give. What's this all about?'

Pride and anger warred within her, and anger finally won. 'I saw you yesterday,' she blurted out. 'With Woody.'

'With Woody?'

'How quickly we forget,' she snapped. 'Yes, with Woody. In your room. You…you were kissing her.'

'Kissing her?' he repeated, then to her absolute fury the bewilderment on his face became amusement—amusement and delight. 'And you're jealous?'

'No, of course I'm not jealous,' she spluttered. 'I just happen to think that if a man kisses a girl on Saturday—asks if he can see her again—he might at least have the decency to wait more than five days before he's groping someone else.'

'I don't grope—never have. Annie, you're an idiot. Yes, I kissed Woody but—'

'This had better be good, Gideon,' Tom commented as he came down the corridor towards them. 'I've got masses of paperwork to catch up on and the last thing I need is an unexpected staff meeting.' He glanced from Annie's furious face to Gideon's exasperated one, and his eyebrows rose. 'You did say three o'clock, didn't you?'

'Am I late?' Helen gasped, racing out of the door which led to the stairs. 'I got held up in Haematology—'

'Nobody's late,' Gideon interrupted, 'and this won't take long. In fact, if you could all take a seat in my room, we'll get started.'

'Shouldn't we wait for Woody?' Helen asked, and Gideon shook his head.

'She's not in today, which is one of the reasons I've called this meeting, but I'll explain about that in a minute. Firstly I'm afraid we're going to have a visitation tomorrow. The government in its wisdom has set up a team of consultant obs and gynae experts and is sending them off to visit hospitals all over the country to check out standards and procedures.'

'Oh, terrific—that's all we need,' Tom groaned. 'Some expert poking about the department, telling us how things should be done and conveniently forgetting that we have to work within the limitations of what we've got. Who is this bloke, and how long is he going to be inflicted upon us?'

'I'm afraid I can't give you his name,' Gideon replied, 'but he's going to be with us for a week or so. Which brings me to the second reason for this meeting,' he continued, as Tom began to mutter darkly about government experts simply being consultants who couldn't hack it in the real world. 'Woody's aunt died of motor neurone disease last week, and she's asked if she can take some compassionate leave to sort everything out.'

They all looked at one another uncertainly, and Annie wondered if she was the only one who hadn't known that Woody had an aunt, ill or otherwise.

'I don't mean to sound hard or unfeeling, Gideon,' Tom said awkwardly, 'but how much leave are we talking about here? Two or three weeks...'

'Three months. Yes, I know,' Gideon said, as they all gazed at him with dismay. 'It's going to leave us drastically short-staffed, but I could hardly say no. Woody's never taken her full holiday entitlement, and her aunt's death has affected her badly.'

'Her parents both died when she was young, didn't they?' Helen frowned, and Gideon nodded.

'Apparently this aunt was the only family she had, and why she didn't tell anyone is beyond me. Motor neurone's a hell of a disease, and to think of her working here, then going home and having to look after the poor woman... I only got the full facts out of her last night when she broke down in my room, and I had to comfort her.'

Gideon's eyes were fixed on Annie as he spoke, and a dull flush of mortified colour crept across her cheeks. No wonder the specialist registrar had been in his arms yesterday. No wonder Woody had looked so exhausted and thin recently, and she'd stupidly thought the two of them were having an affair.

'Gideon, I don't see how we're going to manage without her,' Helen protested. 'We're already postponing ops because our schedules are so full.'

He nodded. 'I know it's going to be difficult, but the trouble is, we haven't a hope in hell of getting somebody to fill in during her leave of absence.'

'Actually, we might be able to get someone,' Tom said thoughtfully. 'An old med school friend of mine has been working in Australia for the past ten years and he's taking up a post in Canada in the summer. I understand he's planning to visit some of his old haunts in Britain for a couple of months, but if I lean on him gently I might be able to persuade him to do Woody's job instead.'

'I don't remember you ever talking about an old med friend who'd gone to Australia.' Helen frowned, and her husband grinned.

'That's because he and I used to get up to the kind of things at med school I wouldn't want my wife to know about.'

'If you could contact him for me I'd be really grateful,' Gideon said as Helen laughed, 'but in the meantime I'm afraid it looks like long hours and precious little time off for any of us.'

There were collective groans all round but as Helen and Tom headed out the door and Annie made to follow them, Gideon caught her arm firmly.

'Not so fast, young lady. I think you owe me an apology, don't you?'

She did, but she wasn't about to take all the blame.

'What was I supposed to think?' she said defensively. 'When I saw you kissing her—heard you'd bought two tickets for the ball tonight—'

'I bought two tickets because I was hoping you'd be my date for this evening.'

'Me?' she said faintly. 'But—'

'Annie, I know you're scared of getting involved with anyone again. Hell, I'm scared, too, but every time we've kissed…' He raked his fingers through his brown hair and smiled. A slightly crooked, rueful smile. 'When Susan died I thought I could never be attracted to another woman again, but then you came into my life, and… Come with me to the ball tonight, Annie. Please.'

She wanted to go with him—she really wanted to go—but… 'I'll never be able to get a babysitter at such short notice, Gideon.'

'David said he'd watch Jamie for you.'

'David?' she echoed. 'You've spoken to my brother about this?'

Gideon looked a little shamefaced. 'Well, I had to ring him about something else…'

'Oh, really?'

'And I just happened to mention that the hospital was holding a dance tonight, and he said he wasn't working this evening and he'd nothing planned so he'd be more than happy to babysit.'

Her brother without a date on a Friday night—and not just any night but St Valentine's night? No way. Never. He'd cancelled. For her, he'd cancelled.

'No pressure, Annie,' Gideon continued, watching her. 'We'll take it slowly—one step at a time—and we won't be alone tonight. There'll probably be over a hundred and fifty couples at the ball so we'll just dance a few dances—'

'I've got two left feet—'

'Then we'll shuffle about together a bit.'

'I've only got one posh dress—'

'I'm sure you'll look beautiful in it. Please, Annie. I would very much like you to come.'

Helen would never let her hear the end of it. Neither would Liz. She'd have days—probably weeks—of questions to answer, speculation to endure, but Gideon looked suddenly so very vulnerable. Vulnerable, and uncertain, and before she could stop herself she said, 'All right. I'll come.'

CHAPTER EIGHT

'MUMMY, you look like a fairy princess.'

'Why, thank you, sweetheart.' Annie laughed as her son gazed up at her in wide-eyed, frank admiration.

'Actually, the boy's quite right,' David commented, his eyes taking in her blue silk dress with its tiny puffed sleeves, fitted waist and wide, floor-length skirt. 'You do look pretty good.'

'You don't think it's too tight?' she asked, fastening the heart-shaped crystal pendant he'd given her for her birthday. 'I haven't worn this since before Jamie was born, and my waistline's a lot bigger now—'

'Annie, when Gideon Caldwell sees you in that it'll blow his socks off.'

She didn't know about blowing his socks off, but she did know she'd never got ready to go out in such a rush before.

Not arriving home until after five o'clock hadn't helped. Mrs Simpson had been violently sick when she'd come round from the anaesthetic following her hysterectomy, then Sylvia Renton's husband had wanted a word that had stretched to a full forty minutes of reassurance about his son, and then she'd had to placate the day-care centre when she'd arrived late yet again.

Luckily David had arrived early for his babysitting duties, but with Jamie running in and out of the bedroom to see what she was doing, and then discovering she'd had to breathe in really hard to get into her one and only evening dress, it was a wonder she didn't look like a frazzled wreck.

Actually, she did look like a frazzled wreck, she

thought as she gazed at herself in the sitting-room mirror. There'd been no time to go to the hairdresser's so she'd washed and blow-dried her hair at home. Nine tenths of the time it would have come out perfectly, but this time— the time it really mattered—her wayward curls just wouldn't lie the way she wanted them to. And then she'd blinked just after she'd finished applying her mascara, and everyone knew it was never the same when you did it again.

'Trust me, love, you look gorgeous,' David murmured, clearly reading her thoughts.

'I'll settle for halfway OK,' she said with a shaky laugh, then jumped when her front doorbell rang. 'That'll be Gideon. Could you let him in for me? I…I've got to collect my handbag.'

It was the truth, but not the whole truth. She needed those extra few seconds to calm herself.

Lord, but she was as nervous as a teenager on her first date, she realised, smoothing down her dress and noticing that her hands were shaking. And that was the trouble. This was a date. Not a simple visit to the park with Jamie, but a real, honest-to-goodness date.

Before, they'd had Jamie to focus on, to distract and divert them, but this time she would be on her own.

What if they found they had nothing to talk about? What if Gideon discovered she was actually as boring as hell without her son, with no conversation or interests outside medicine? She should have said no. She should have said he'd given her far too little time to get ready, but now he was here, and it was too late. Too late to change her mind.

'Prince Charming's here.'

She turned vexedly to tell David to stop playing the fool, only for the words to die in her throat when she saw Gideon standing beside him. Somebody had once told her there wasn't a man born who couldn't be transformed into a handsome prince by evening dress or a kilt. She hadn't believed them. She believed it now.

Dressed in a dark evening suit, with an immaculate white shirt, crisp bow-tie and his hair neatly brushed down, he didn't look like Gideon Caldwell at all. He looked handsome, and desirable, and all the things she'd once thought he wasn't, and she was doubly convinced that her dress was too tight and her hair was all wrong.

'You…you look very nice, Annie,' he murmured.

'*Nice?*' David protested. 'Good grief, man, she looks terrific. Wonderful. Drop-dead gorgeous.'

Gideon flushed, and raked a hand through his hair so it wasn't smooth any more but stood a little bit on end like it always did at work, and suddenly he was the Gideon Caldwell she knew again. The Gideon Caldwell of the rough tweed jacket and the shirt with the button missing. The Gideon Caldwell she'd liked from the very first moment she'd met him. She smiled shyly.

'I…I think you look very nice, too,' she said.

David threw his eyes heavenwards as though to say he washed his hands of the pair of them, but Gideon didn't seem to notice. His lips curved, and he said, 'I'm afraid I can't offer you a glass carriage, but my ever so slightly rusty Peugeot is ready whenever you are.'

He helped her on with her coat, his hands briefly squeezing her shoulders, and she knew that she didn't need a carriage. He was enough. More than enough.

'Have a nice time,' David said. 'And don't do anything I wouldn't. Which pretty much gives the pair of you carte blanche to do anything.'

'Just make sure Jamie's in bed at a reasonable hour,' Annie replied pointedly. 'I know what he's like—and I know what you're like—and I don't want to come home and discover he's still up.'

'Oh, you won't.' David beamed. 'That I can positively guarantee.'

For a second she had the strangest feeling he was up to something, but then Jamie grabbed her round the knees and hugged her.

'I still think you look like a fairy princess,' he whispered, and her throat closed, and she hugged him back.

She felt like one, too, as Gideon escorted her down to his car. She felt strange, and unreal, and excited, all at the same time.

It was only when they arrived at the Grosvenor Hotel, and she saw the happy throng of Belfield staff going in, that a momentary doubt assailed her.

'You do realise we're never going to hear the end of this, don't you?' she said as Gideon switched off his ignition. 'The minute we walk in that door every tongue in the place is going to wag, and what they don't know they're going to make up.'

He turned to her, his face ruggedly handsome in the streetlight, and smiled. 'You know something? Right now, I don't give a damn.'

Neither did she. Not even when Liz collared her as she hung up her coat and said, 'Talk about dark horses, Annie Hart.'

And Helen grabbed her hand and said, 'I'm so pleased. Oh, I can't tell you how pleased I am.'

Everything about this evening seemed unreal-magical. From the fairy-tale lights and heart-shaped balloons strung over the function room to the finger buffet and the sparkling wine. From the speech from the head of Admin, welcoming everyone to the event, to the potent love songs the band was playing.

And Gideon. Always there was Gideon, looking incredibly handsome and desirable in his evening suit. Gideon constantly by her side, identifying the people she didn't know. Gideon's eyes fixed on her so tenderly, making her feel special, and cared for, and cherished.

Which was why she didn't even make a token protest

when he urged her out onto the dance floor. Why, when he slid one hand round her waist and captured her hand against his heart, drawing her close to him so that her head just fitted against his shoulder, she didn't remember one very important thing.

'You weren't kidding, were you, when you said you had two left feet?' he murmured, wincing slightly after she'd stood on his foot yet again.

'I'm sorry,' she said in consternation. 'Do you want to forget this—sit down again?'

'Not on your life.' He grinned. 'Cinderella's got to have at least one flaw, and if trampling on my feet is her only one, I can live with it.'

And she laughed and let him draw her firmly back into his arms, and felt the magic and wonder of the evening engulf her again.

How had she got to be this lucky? Meeting somebody like Gideon when she'd been so sure—so determined—she would live out the rest of her life alone? Now suddenly the world was full of wonderful possibilities.

And feelings, too, she realised, when he refused to release her after the music stopped but wanted to dance with her again, and again. Holding her closer and closer to him with every dance, heedless of her awkward feet, moulding his body to hers, so that she could feel the uneven throb of his heartbeat, could see his eyes growing darker and more intense with every passing second.

So much for taking it one step at a time, she thought, sighing against his shoulder when she felt his lips brush her hair. So much for her determination to be independent, to never let a man into her life again.

It was all gone, she realised as she lifted her head and stared up at him and saw the need and desire in his eyes. Gone in this man's arms. Gone because he was Gideon, and she wanted him.

'Hey, some of us came here to dance,' somebody protested, and they drew apart quickly, Annie not knowing whose cheeks were redder—hers or Gideon's.

Lord, he'd said they wouldn't be alone tonight, but they might just as well have been for all the notice they'd been taking of anybody else.

'I think I'd better drive you home before I completely forget myself,' Gideon said with a shaky laugh, clearly mirroring her thoughts.

She managed to laugh, too, but she didn't want to leave. Didn't want this magical evening to end. David would be at home, waiting to grill her, and she wanted to hold onto these wonderful precious feelings for just a little while longer. Wanted to postpone his inquisition, and the even bigger inquisition she knew she'd undoubtedly face from her colleagues tomorrow.

But she couldn't. It was almost midnight, and even Cinderella hadn't been permitted to enjoy her evening beyond that.

'I'll get my coat,' she said reluctantly, and his fingers tightened briefly round her hand, then he nodded.

To her relief, she didn't meet anybody she knew on her way to the cloakroom. In fact, the foyer and bar were deserted except for Tom and a group of other doctors, but as they were all clustered round the hotel TV she knew she was safe from an inquisition for the moment.

'Good game?' she couldn't resist saying just for devilment, and saw Tom's head snap round guiltily.

'Terrific, Annie,' he enthused, relief plain on his face when he realised it was her. 'One goal each, two cracking shots at the crossbar, and there's still another fifteen minutes to go.'

And Helen will kill you if she finds you here, Annie thought with a wry inward chuckle.

Would she and Gideon eventually become like that? she wondered as she retrieved her coat. He being more interested in watching a football match than in dancing with her?

Whoa, there, she told herself, catching sight of her flushed cheeks, her bright eyes, in the cloakroom mirror. Slow down. Who's rushing now? This is your first proper date with the man. A date that's going to end when he takes you home.

Which was probably just as well, she thought as Gideon drove her through the dark city streets and she sat beside him acutely and painfully aware of his presence. Everything was moving much too fast, and it was just as well David and Jamie were going to be there to put the brakes on.

Except that they weren't.

'Have decided to take Jamie back to my place,' David had written on a piece of paper taped to the mantelpiece. 'After all, two's company, and four's most definitely a crowd. I'll drop him off at the day care centre for you tomorrow so why don't you and Gideon take the opportunity to really get to know one another?'

'Do you want to kill him, or will I?' Annie said.

'He means well.'

'That's the story of my brother's life.'

Gideon chuckled. A warm deep sound that made the sitting room seem even quieter than it had been before. Made him seem altogether much bigger and a hell of a lot more immediate than he'd done before.

Oh, lord, but she'd been the one who'd wanted the evening to never end. She should have been careful what she'd wished for.

'Would you like a cup of coffee before you go?' she blurted out, then flushed when she realised how that must sound. 'Not that I'm asking you to go— I mean, I'm not throwing you out or anything—'

'Annie, I know what you mean,' he said gently. 'And a cup of coffee would be lovely.'

She didn't know about lovely but at least it would give her something to do. Some time to calm her skittering heart. Some time to get her jumbled thoughts and feelings into order, and to forget the implication in David's letter.

'One cup of coffee coming up,' she said brightly, much too brightly, when she carried the mugs into the sitting room.

Gideon was sitting on the sofa. For a second she hesitated but it would look odd if she sat way over by the fireplace so she sat down on the sofa, too, thanking her lucky stars that her landlady had provided a three-seater because at least it meant there was a wide, comforting gap between them.

'Nice coffee,' Gideon observed, taking a sip.

'It's just instant. David gave me a percolator but I've never quite got the hang of it, and it takes for ever to heat.'

He nodded, and she felt like an idiot. Babbling on about coffee and percolators, but her brain felt like a sieve. Her brain totally emptied when he undid his bow-tie, then the top button of his shirt.

'That's better,' he said with a sigh of relief, rolling and stretching his neck. 'I've been feeling half-strangled all night. Whoever designed bow-ties and high starched collars should have been shot.'

Or given a medal, she thought, trying very hard not to notice the tantalising V of dark, silky hair he'd exposed.

'I…I expect Jamie will be as high as a kite tomorrow,' she said with a little laugh. 'He's not used to late hours and David will never think of putting him to bed at a reasonable hour.'

'I don't think one late night will do him any harm.'

'I guess not.'

She took a gulp of her coffee, and then another. 'Do you—?'

'Have you—?'

They'd spoken together, and he smiled. 'You first.'

'I was only— I was just going to say I hope the visiting consultant doesn't give you too much hassle.'

'I expect I'll survive.'

Which pretty well ended that as a topic of conversation, she thought, and it wasn't a topic of conversation for a night like this anyway. It was stupid, and irrelevant, and boring.

Say something clever and witty, Annie, she urged herself. If she didn't, he was going to think she was about as interesting as yesterday's news, but the trouble was she was, so nervous. Nervous of saying the wrong thing, doing the wrong thing, looking like an idiot.

'What…what were you going to say before I interrupted you?' she asked in desperation.

'I was just thinking about your brother. He seems very good at organising other people, and yet…'

'He's thirty-two, flits from girlfriend to girlfriend and is currently unattached.' She sighed. 'I don't know what David wants. I don't think he knows either.'

'Do you?'

His eyes were fixed on her and her heart seemed to be suddenly jammed in her throat, making it hard for her to breathe, hard to do anything.

'I… Would…would you like another coffee?' she said. 'It won't take me long to boil the kettle again, and—'

He caught her hand in his before she could move, and laced her fingers in his.

'Annie, irrespective of your brother's suggestion, nothing is going to happen tonight that you don't want or feel comfortable with, OK?'

His voice was deep, velvety in the stillness, and she stared down at their meshed fingers and swallowed, hard.

'I know that, but I…I don't know what I want. At least I do—sort of—but it's been four years, and the thought of—'

'Annie, look at me.'

Slowly she lifted her head. There was understanding in Gideon's eyes. Understanding and, to her surprise, uncertainty, too.

He was as nervous and as unsure about this as she was, she suddenly realised, and that gave her the courage to whisper, 'Hold me, Gideon.'

He drew her into his arms, held her against him so that she could feel his thundering heartbeat and then kissed her. Gently at first, teasing her lips apart to open for him, and then more thoroughly, and heat began to build in her. A low, throbbing heat that started at the pit of her stomach, then rippled out in wave after wave of aching desire.

I want him, she thought as she threaded her fingers through his hair, returning his kisses with a depth to match his own. I want him, she realised as his fingers came up and cupped her breast, his palm hot and hard through the fine silk of her dress.

'Oh, Annie, tell me to stop,' he said hoarsely against her cheek, 'because if we do this for much longer I'm not going to be able to stop.'

She didn't want him to. She felt alive with longing, and wanting, and the last thing she wanted was for him to stop.

'Make love to me, Gideon,' she said.

'Are you sure?' he asked, his voice ragged, uneven. 'Annie, I want you. I want you so much, but I need you to be sure—for you to have no regrets.'

Her only regret was that she hadn't met him sooner, she realised as she led him through to her bedroom and he gently took off her clothes and then his own, but she wouldn't have had Jamie if she had, and she could never regret him.

With their clothes gone, there was no time for regrets anyway. No time for anything but the joy and wonder of holding him, of having him hold her. Of the feel of his hard, masculine strength against her as he lowered her to the bed, the touch of his hands and lips, caressing, coaxing, teasing, so that the heat began again, spiralling and spiralling, until she was pleading, 'Now, Gideon, take me now.'

And he did, balancing himself on his forearms as he entered her, driving slowly at first, then faster and faster, his breathing harsh and unsteady in her hair as she moved beneath him, arching her hips against him, striving to reach the final culmination, and then suddenly the whole world exploded and she screamed out his name and her entire body convulsed around him.

A few seconds later he gave a low guttural cry, and his whole body shuddered and jerked against her as he reached his own climax, then he laid his head on the pillow beside her and she held him as he spilled deep within her.

'Are you all right?' he asked gruffly when he eventually lifted his head, and she nodded back at him wordlessly.

All right? Wonderful would have been closer to the truth. Wonderful, and fulfilled, and stupidly—ridiculously—close to tears.

As though sensing it, he rolled over carefully, taking her with him so her head was cradled on his chest.

'All the way over here in the car I kept telling myself, Take it slowly, Gideon, don't pressurise her,' he said softly. 'But then…'

'I know,' she murmured. 'Gideon…'

'This is just the start, Annie,' he said, kissing her hair and holding her tight. 'For you and me, this is just the start.'

And as she drifted off to sleep in his arms, she believed him.

It was dawn when Annie woke. Four years of motherhood had got her into the habit of waking early, but when she opened her eyes and saw her clothes lying scattered about the bedroom the last thing she felt like was a mother.

Gideon had gone, of course. Some time during the night he'd woken her and made love to her again, and then he'd told her he would have to leave early for the Belfield. The government bigwig was due that day, and he wouldn't put it past him to arrive early.

She sighed and turned over, not wanting to get up but wanting to hold onto the memory of last night for just a little longer, and blinked.

There was a flower by her pillow. A winter pansy. For a second she wondered where on earth he could possibly have got it until she remembered her landlady had a whole border full, and a laugh escaped her. A laugh that warmed and cheered her as she reluctantly got out of bed to get ready for work. A laugh she was all too aware she was going to need when she reached the hospital, and the inquisition began about her presence at the dance with Gideon.

But not immediately, she realised when she opened the door to Obs and Gynae and almost fell over a sweeper and two cleaning ladies.

'What the—?'

'I know—I know,' Liz said, seeing her, 'but it's got nothing to do with me. The powers that be upstairs have decided that in honour of our visiting consultant we've got to look like one of those glossy adverts for the NHS instead of the grim reality.'

'What's he like, this consultant?' Annie asked, carefully sidestepping one of the cleaners.

'No idea. He arrived before I started my shift, and he's been closeted with Gideon in his consulting room ever since.'

Damn, and she'd wanted to have a word with him to thank him for the flower, and just simply to see him again.

'And talking about being closeted,' Liz continued, her

eyes gleaming. 'What's this with you and Gideon? I want all the gory details of how you got together, when you became an item. I want everything.'

So did Helen. So did practically every patient on the ward. Quite how they'd all got to know she'd been Gideon's partner for the St Valentine's Ball was beyond her, though she could have made a pretty shrewd guess.

'I'm just so very pleased for you and Mr Caldwell.' Jennifer beamed, clearly already mentally booking the wedding reception and honeymoon. 'He's such a lovely man, isn't he—such a very special man? He deserves to be happy.'

And Annie muttered something incoherent in reply, and was wondering if her cheeks would ever return to their normal colour again when Kay said the same thing. Mrs Simpson, who had only been in the place five minutes did, too.

Sylvia was the only patient she managed to have anything like a near normal conversation with, but that gave her no pleasure at all.

'I don't want to disturb the nurses and doctors in the intensive care baby unit,' she said when Annie asked her if she'd visited her son that morning. 'And I'm feeling a bit tired today.'

'I could get one of the porters to wheel you along there,' Annie suggested. 'And you most certainly wouldn't be disturbing anyone. In fact, I'm sure they'll be delighted to see you.'

'Perhaps later,' Sylvia muttered. 'After lunch.'

And perhaps never if nobody forced her, Annie thought with a deep sigh. She'd have to speak to Gideon about the woman, visiting consultant or no visiting consultant.

'Hey, what's wrong with my favourite junior doctor?' a deep, velvety voice murmured behind her. 'She's looking decidedly down in the mouth, and we certainly can't have that.'

She turned to see Gideon smiling down at her, and felt a slow blush of colour covering her cheeks as she realised that every eye on the ward was fixed on them, and every ear was straining to catch their conversation.

'Could I have a word with you in private, please, Mr Caldwell?' she asked.

'In private?' he echoed, puzzled.

'I think it might be better, don't you?' she said pointedly, shooting a glance sideways towards Kay, who was obviously hanging on their every word, and Liz, who appeared to be taking an inordinate interest in the chart on the end of Mrs Simpson's bed.

'Ah. Right.' He nodded. 'Come with me, Dr Hart.'

A collective sigh of disappointment went up from the ward as she followed him out into the corridor, and by the time the door was safely closed his cheeks were almost as dark as hers.

'Good grief, has it been like this all morning?'

'Think yourself lucky you're stuck with the government man,' she said. 'I thought my brother was bad enough, but this lot…'

'Are you sorry about last night?'

His eyes caught and held hers, and she shook her head. 'Not a bit. Thank goodness they only know we went to the dance together, because if they knew about the rest…'

He chuckled, glanced over his shoulder, then bent his head and kissed her. A kiss that was all too tantalisingly brief. 'On account,' he murmured when she protested.

'Can I see you tonight?' she asked. 'I could ask David if he'd mind babysitting again…'

'I'm afraid I can't. In fact, it looks like I'm going to be stuck with our visiting consultant until he leaves.'

'He expects you to work nights?' she gasped.

'There's really no other time we can get through all the data he wants to see unless I give up operating and doing any ward rounds during the day, which isn't a practical option.' He cupped her chin in his hand and smiled as she gazed at him unhappily. 'One week. Ten days tops, Annie, and then…'

'I'd far rather have the "and then" now,' she said wistfully, and he laughed.

'So would I.'

'What's he like—this slave-driving consultant?' she asked after he'd kissed her again, this time not nearly so briefly.

'Younger than I'd thought. Tall, blond, handsome. In fact, I guarantee every woman in the hospital will be half in love with him by the beginning of next week.'

'Not this one,' she replied. 'This woman prefers the tall, dark, brown-haired type.'

'I'm glad to hear it,' he said, his lips quirking, then he sighed. 'I've got to go. I only stepped out for a breather from all the facts and figures. Did you really want to talk to me, or were you just wanting an escape, too?'

She shook her head, and quickly told him about Sylvia.

'OK, I'll phone the hospital psychiatrist right away, and have him come down. The quicker this is resolved, the better.'

The quicker the visiting consultant left, the better, Annie thought as she watched Gideon disappear down the corridor.

Ten days. It sounded like a lifetime, but she could wait. She'd already waited a lifetime for a man like Gideon Caldwell, so she could wait a little longer.

The rest of the morning sped by in an exhausting round of examinations and note-taking. It wasn't helped, of course, by the fact that they were now two doctors short on the ward instead of just one, but luckily no major emergency developed so at least she and Liz were able to grab their afternoon coffee-break before they went back into the fray.

Not that she got much relaxation over her coffee. Not

with Liz quizzing her about the whys and wherefores of her turning out to be Gideon's mysterious partner for the St Valentine's Ball.

'I just hope it works out for the two of you—I really do,' the sister declared as she led the way back to the ward. 'Gideon deserves the best, and so do you.'

Right now Gideon needed a rest, Annie decided, seeing him at the top of the ward, talking to a tall, blond-haired man. He looked tired, and harassed, and she wasn't surprised. An entire morning spent discussing facts and figures with some visiting bigwig couldn't have been much fun. Especially as he hadn't got much sleep last night, she realised, colouring slightly at the memory, only for every trace of colour in her face to instantly disappear when the blond man suddenly turned round.

'Wowee,' Liz breathed beside her. 'Who is that, and can I have him gift-wrapped, please?'

Annie had thought the same when she'd first met Nick Henderson at the Manchester Infirmary. Had thought him the handsomest man she'd ever seen. He was still handsome, she noticed, his blond hair gleaming under the ward's fluorescent lights, and she felt physically sick.

'Oh, terrific! Gideon's going to introduce him,' Liz exclaimed with delight, her fingers automatically going up to tidy her red curls. 'Now, hands off, Annie. I saw him first.'

And she wanted to crawl into a hole and stay there, Annie thought as she saw recognition slowly dawn on Nick's face as he came down the ward towards her. She wanted to run out the door and never come back. But most of all she wanted to know why he had to come back into her life now, just when she was about to get it together.

'I don't believe it,' Nick said, reaching out to grasp both her hands the minute they'd drawn level. 'Annie Hart. Good grief, I haven't seen you in— Good heavens, it must be almost five years.'

Four years and four months to be exact, she thought. Not that she was counting. Like hell she wasn't.

'Hello, Mr Henderson,' she said, extracting her hands deliberately, and Nick smiled. The smile which had once been able to turn her knees to water. They weren't water now, but they were none too steady either.

'Hello yourself, Annie,' he said warmly, then turned to Gideon with an even bigger smile. 'Sorry about this, Mr Caldwell, but Annie and I knew each other years ago at the Manchester Infirmary.'

'I see,' Gideon murmured.

'Annie Hart.' Nick shook his head in amazement, as though her appearance was as delightful and as unexpected as an unscheduled visit from Halley's comet. 'I still can't believe it. Here of all places. We must have dinner together one evening. Talk about old times.'

Like hell they would. 'How's your wife?' she asked, and saw his smile slip momentarily.

'I'm afraid Lucy and I divorced a couple of years ago. These things happen, but at least we parted amicably.'

And pigs might fly. He'd always said Lucy hadn't understood him, but it looked like she'd finally wised up.

'Do you still want to take a look at the patient input levels for last year, Mr Henderson?' Gideon asked. 'Or would you rather—?'

'Oh, we'd better get to the figures. That's what I'm here for after all,' Nick said expansively. 'But I won't forget about that dinner date, Annie. You can depend on it.'

She didn't give a damn about his dinner date. She didn't give a damn about him, but what she did care about—deeply cared about—was the puzzled, questioning look Gideon gave her as he walked away with Nick.

CHAPTER NINE

'I WANT a holiday,' Liz declared when Annie arrived in the staffroom for the start of her morning shift. 'Better yet, I want a transfer.'

'Things rough again this morning?' Annie murmured as she hung up her coat.

'If you mean are Helen and Tom still running around like headless chickens, and is Gideon still snapping at everything and anyone that moves, then, yes, things are rough.'

Five days, Annie thought as she reached for her white coat. Nick had only arrived at the Belfield five days ago, and yet gone was the happy, relaxed atmosphere which had once been so characteristic of the obs and gynae ward, and in its place was discord and unhappiness.

It had been inevitable, of course. Nobody liked their work examined and criticised, or being forced to endure time-and-motion studies to see if their work could be performed more efficiently, but the problems that Nick's arrival had caused were much deeper than that, far deeper.

'Are you quite sure you and Gideon haven't had a row?' Liz continued, watching Annie as she put her stethoscope in her pocket, checked her notebook, then dragged a brush quickly through her hair. 'I know this Henderson bloke has been hassling him about the numbers of operations we perform, and patients we see at the clinics and Outpatients, but the way Gideon's been behaving lately… It's not like him. It's not like him at all.'

It wasn't, Annie thought irritably, and the trouble was, everyone thought they'd had a row. Even the patients out on the ward.

'Never let the sun go down on your wrath, Dr Hart,' Mrs Simpson had said pointedly. 'That's what my old mum used to say, and she was married sixty years.'

'I've always found that the secret to a happy relationship is to apologise, even if you're not in the wrong,' Kay had told her, concern plain on her plump face.

Good grief, even Tom had put in his pennyworth when they'd been operating one morning. 'Whatever the problem is, Annie, talk about it. More relationships bite the dust through couples not talking to one another than for any other reason.'

It was good advice. It was terrific advice, but how could you talk to a man who was avoiding you? And Gideon was avoiding her. She knew he was.

At first she'd thought she was just imagining it, that he was simply run off his feet, with Woody being away on compassionate leave and Nick never off his back, but as the days had passed she'd been forced to concede that even a very busy man could have found time to exchange a few words with her. Even a man who was completely snowed under could have found a minute to answer the messages she'd left on his answering machine.

It's the brush-off, Annie, her mind whispered as she reluctantly followed Liz out onto the ward. All he wanted was to make love to you, and now that he has he's not interested any more.

But he wasn't like that, her heart protested. When they'd made love… Oh, when they'd made love it had been the most wonderful night of her life, and he couldn't have been faking his own reaction—simply couldn't.

Nick did, the insidious little voice pointed out. Nick was prepared to swear undying love to get you into his bed. Gideon didn't even do that. All he said was that this was the beginning for you and him, which could have meant anything and nothing.

But she couldn't have got it wrong again, she thought,

trying hard to ignore the sympathetic glances that were coming from the patients. OK, so she made a mistake in the past, but surely she couldn't have made a mistake again.

'One new admission last night,' Helen told her, her face drawn, harassed. 'Joy Turner, thirty-seven weeks pregnant. Her GP sent her in as a precaution because her BP's up and her ankles are very swollen. Her diastolic is still slightly less than 100, so if it is pre-eclampsia, it's pretty mild.'

'Better safe than sorry,' Annie commented, and the SHO nodded, only to bite her lip and groan.

'Cripes. He-who-must-now-be-instantly-obeyed has just arrived, and I'm out of here.'

Annie wished she could bolt, too, when she turned to see Gideon striding through the swing doors at the end of the ward for the start of his morning round. He looked tired and harassed, but most of all he looked angry.

'Sister Baker, this ward is a disgrace.'

'A disgrace?' Liz echoed faintly.

'Discarded magazines lying about, wilting flowers, dirty teacups—it's not good enough.'

Hot colour swept across Liz's cheeks. 'I'm sorry, Mr Caldwell. It won't happen again.'

'See that it doesn't,' he ordered. 'Dr Hart, if you're ready?'

He didn't even wait for her reply. He simply strode across to Mrs Simpson's bed and waited, impatience and irritation plain on his face.

'Remember that holiday I was mentioning?' Liz murmured as she and Annie hurried towards him. 'Forget it. I want the transfer. Now.'

Annie wanted some answers. Annie wished she possessed the courage simply to walk up to him and say, 'Gideon, we made love less than a week ago, and I thought we shared something special, but you haven't returned my calls, and you're ignoring me at work, so are you giving me the brush-off, or what?'

But she couldn't say it. Lord, just thinking about actually saying it was enough to make her cringe inwardly, which left her… Precisely nowhere.

'I want Mrs Simpson's antibiotics doubled, and a two-hourly examination made of the incision,' Gideon declared once he'd finished his examination. 'There's definite signs of a localised infection, and if it shows any sign of spreading I want to know about it immediately.'

'Is something wrong?' Mrs Simpson asked, glancing from him to Liz as the girl nodded. 'This localised infection…'

'I think you could have an allergy to the suturing materials I used during your operation,' Gideon explained. 'If you do, the inflammation will disappear once your stitches are removed, but there's also the slight chance you might have an infection.'

'But—'

'I haven't lost a hysterectomy patient yet, Mrs Simpson,' he smiled, 'and you're not going to be the first.'

Annie smiled, too, as Mrs Simpson let out a sigh of relief. That was one thing Nick's arrival hadn't changed— Gideon's ability to say just the right thing to a patient. He might be running Helen and Tom ragged and avoiding her like the plague, but he always had time for his patients. Which was why she was totally unprepared for him to suddenly spin round.

'I…I'm sorry,' she gasped as they collided.

'It's my fault,' he said brusquely. 'I wasn't looking where I was going.'

'Isn't that usually my line?' she murmured without thinking, only to flush scarlet when she realised he'd heard.

Oh, cripes. In the changed atmosphere of Obs and Gynae a flip comment like that was most certainly going to earn her an earful, but to her surprise he didn't look angry. In fact—wonder of wonders—the corners of his mouth actually lifted.

'On this occasion the blame was definitely mine,' he said, then his forehead creased when he saw her absently rubbing her elbow. 'Have you hurt yourself?'

She shook her head. 'I just caught my arm on the end of the bed.'

'Let me see.'

'No, really, it's OK,' she declared, realising that Mrs Simpson was listening to their conversation with keen interest. So was Kay. In fact, if Kay had been any more interested, she'd have fallen out of bed. 'It was just a knock, that's all.'

'You're sure?' he pressed.

Oh, even greater wonders, he was actually looking at her. Not at some vague point a little bit above her head, like he'd been doing for the past five days, but actually *at* her. Like he cared, like he was truly worried.

'I'm just a bit slow on my feet this morning, that's all,' she said.

'Actually, you're never particularly light on them, are you?' he said, his brown eyes twinkling, and the colour on her cheeks darkened as she suddenly realised what he was remembering. The dances they'd shared at the St Valentine's Ball.

'Someone… Somebody once told me that everyone was entitled to at least one flaw,' she declared, emboldened by the smile. 'In fact—'

'Morning, everyone—sorry I'm late,' exclaimed a familiar bright voice behind her, and Annie could have wept with frustration when she saw the light and laughter instantly disappear from Gideon's face.

Nick's timing couldn't have been worse. In fact, why did he have to keep on joining them on every ward round at all? Ye gods, surely one tour would have been enough to tell him what everyone who worked at the Belfield already knew: that the department was underfunded, and understaffed. And yet Nick still insisted on joining them every day, poking his nose in, criticising, carping.

'You're not late at all, Mr Henderson,' Gideon said, his voice clipped. 'In fact, we've only just started.'

'Good—good.' Nick beamed. 'Lead on, then, Mr Caldwell, and I'll tag along behind with Annie.'

Which was another thing that was really getting under her skin, Annie thought, seeing Gideon's face tighten further before he walked on to Kay's bed. The way Nick never called her Dr Hart. It was always, 'Annie this' and 'Annie that', as though he was deliberately trying to remind her of how much he'd once meant to her.

Well, she didn't want—or need—reminding. She already knew what a fool she'd been to fall in love with a man who was nothing but a handsome face.

'You can go home as soon as you've arranged for your husband to collect you,' Gideon told a clearly delighted Kay after he'd scanned her chart, 'but I want your promise to take things easy for the next couple of weeks. Get your husband to do any cleaning or cooking, and no dashing out to the shops or going for long walks with the baby.'

'I won't, Mr Caldwell, I promise,' Kay replied, 'and in exchange I want *your* promise to come to Gideon's christening. It won't be anything fancy,' she continued as he began to protest that he hadn't done anything to deserve an invitation, 'but my husband is hoping to get our local pub to give us their upstairs room for the afternoon, and I can definitely promise you a good spread.'

He smiled. 'Sounds like an invitation I can't refuse. OK, send me a card when you've decided on a day, and I'll be there if I can.'

'You must come, too, Dr Hart,' Kay continued, her eyes darting across to Annie. 'My granny always makes far too many sausage rolls when it's a family celebration, so the more mouths to eat them, the better.'

'In that case, it's a pity I'm only going to be here until the middle of next week.' Nick beamed, putting his arm around Annie's shoulder and giving it a squeeze. 'Or I could have come, too. As Annie's partner.'

Never in a million years, Annie thought, shrugging off his arm. I wouldn't walk across the street with you, far less go to a party.

Gideon clearly didn't believe her. Not from his stony-faced expression.

'If you're quite finished, Dr Hart,' he said coldly, 'perhaps we might get on?'

Good grief, surely he didn't think she actually welcomed Nick's cheesy overtures, the way he always seemed to stand just that little bit too close? The only reason she hadn't said anything was because she didn't want to make waves, didn't want Gideon getting any more hassle than he was already receiving, but had her silence suggested she wanted the familiarity? Was that why he'd been behaving so oddly lately? It couldn't be that—surely it couldn't be—but if it was…

If only she could talk to him. If only *he* would talk to her, but as he moved on down the ward, his back ramrod stiff, she knew there was as much chance of that happening as Nick suddenly turning into a half-decent human being.

'Poor Mr Caldwell,' Jennifer said, when Gideon's morning round was finally over and he and Nick had left the ward. 'I feel for him—I really do. He looks so down, doesn't he?'

'We're all a bit tired at the moment,' Annie replied noncommittally. 'What with Dr Dunwoody being on compassionate leave, and—'

'I can't say I think much of this visiting consultant,'

Jennifer sniffed. 'All mouth and trousers, if you want my honest opinion.'

Annie smothered a laugh. 'How are you feeling today?'

'Better. Still terrified witless, of course, at the thought of going home. Every twinge I get, I think, is this it, am I going to lose the other babies? But I know I can't stay here for the rest of my pregnancy.'

'I bet you anything that when you're back here again in six months to have your twins, you'll wonder why on earth you got yourself in such a tizzy,' Annie declared.

'That's what Mr Caldwell says,' Jennifer admitted. 'And speaking of Mr Caldwell, I never did thank you for persuading him to let me stay in for another few days instead of going home on Monday.'

'I didn't do anything,' Annie protested. 'You were just lucky we had a spare bed.'

Jennifer shook her head and smiled. 'You can say what you like, Doctor, but I know what I know.' And then to Annie's surprise she suddenly stretched out and took her hands in hers. 'I don't know what's gone wrong, Dr Hart, and I don't want to know, but I hope it works out for the two of you. I really do.'

Tears filled Annie's eyes and she blinked them away rapidly. Everybody meant well—she knew they did—but they weren't helping. Nothing was going to help until Nick left the Belfield, and then…maybe then Gideon might tell her what she'd said, or done, that had so angered him.

The rest of Annie's shift dragged by in an exhausting round of note-taking, form-filling, chasing up blood results and checking on their new admission.

'I don't know what all the fuss is about, Doctor,' Mrs Turner said with irritation when Annie had taken her blood pressure. 'This will be my fifth, and I never had any trouble with my other babies, but it was a locum GP instead of my regular doctor and he would insist on me coming in.'

'Your blood pressure certainly seems to be stabilising—'

'What did I tell you?' the woman declared triumphantly. 'It's a lot of fuss about nothing.'

I doubt if you'd have thought it was a lot of fuss about nothing if you *had* developed severe pre-eclampsia, Annie thought waspishly, but she didn't say that. Instead, she simply filled in Mrs Turner's chart, clipped it back to the bottom of the bed and left.

An hour to go before she could go home, she thought with a deep sigh as she left the ward and began making her way along to the staffroom. Another hour of sympathetic looks and kindly meant suggestions on how to rekindle her romance with Gideon. Another hour spent hoping she wouldn't walk into Nick, who was fast becoming a complete pain about the dinner date he'd suggested. Maybe instead of politely refusing, she should just be downright rude, and to hell with the consequences.

One thing was certain. She had to look an awful lot more upbeat and happy by the time she got home. She hadn't told David about Nick or Gideon, but he knew something was wrong. He'd been sniffing about for days, trying to get her to talk, but this wasn't something she intended sharing with him. Not even if he put lighted matchsticks under her fingernails.

The door at the end of the corridor clattered open, and her heart sank. Please, let it not be Nick. Not Nick, all cheerful and hail-fellow-well-met. She wasn't in the mood this afternoon, but it wasn't Nick who began walking towards her. It was Louise Harper's boyfriend, the boyfriend Gideon had thrown out of the hospital over a fortnight ago. As he advanced towards her, all her instincts told her she was in trouble.

'Mike—it is Mike, isn't it?' she said hesitantly. 'I'm

afraid Louise isn't here. She's been discharged, and if you're wanting her address—'

'I'm not looking for Louise,' he interrupted harshly. 'You're the one I'm looking for. You're the meddling bitch who told everyone I had gonorrhoea. Louise would never have told anyone what was wrong with her if you hadn't said I needed treatment. There's nothing wrong with me. I'm clean. If I've got gonorrhoea, it's that slag who's given it to me.'

Lord, but where was the panic button? At the Manchester Infirmary there'd been panic buttons everywhere, and there had to be one here, but where in heaven's name was it?

'Look, why don't we go to the staffroom?' she suggested as evenly as her thudding heart would allow. Please, God, Tom might be in there, or Gideon, or even Nick. She'd settle even for Nick at the moment, though how much use he'd be in a crisis was anybody's guess. 'It would be much more comfortable there, and I could make you a cup of tea—coffee—'

'I don't want any of your bloody coffee,' Mike retorted. 'It's time somebody taught you a lesson, lady. It's time somebody taught you to keep your nose out of things that don't concern you.'

Was he drunk? His speech certainly sounded slightly slurred, and his eyes were definitely far too bright. Drunk or on drugs, for sure, she decided, only to cease to care when a knife suddenly appeared in his hands.

With a sharp cry Annie turned on her heel, but she wasn't quick enough. Before she could even move a step he'd grabbed her by the arm, slammed her against the wall and held the knife just inches from her throat.

'You're not going anywhere, lady.' He grinned, his breath hot against her face. 'Except for in a wooden box.'

He was going to kill her. He was going to kill her, and there was nothing she could do about it. He was going to kill her, and Jamie was going to be left motherless as well as fatherless.

Please, oh, please, she prayed, let somebody come. A porter. A lab technician. Normally, the department was overrun with both, but this afternoon…

The door at the end of the corridor banged open again, and she held her breath. Not one of the patients. Please, don't let it be one of the patients. It wasn't. It was Gideon. Gideon, who had taken in the situation in a glance, judging by his sharp intake of breath, but what could he do—what could anybody do?

'There you are, Dr Hart,' he said with apparent irritation. 'I need to see you in my room immediately.'

'I…I'm afraid I'm a bit tied up at the moment, Mr Caldwell,' she replied, then had to bite down hard on her lip because her reply suddenly struck her as hysterically funny, and she knew if she started to laugh she *would* have hysterics.

'And I'm afraid it doesn't matter how busy you are, Dr Hart,' Gideon continued, walking slowly down the corridor towards them. 'I need to speak to you and I need to speak to you now.'

He was talking for talking's sake—buying himself time to get closer—and tentatively she tried to pull her arm out of Mike's grasp, but he only tightened it further.

'I…I have to go, Mike,' she said. 'My boss—you heard what he said…'

He wavered for just a second, and that second was all Gideon needed. With a speed that was startling for such a big man he lunged at Mike, knocking the knife to the floor with one hand and using the other to pinion him with a tight arm lock.

'The panic button, Annie,' he gasped. 'Press the panic button beside the toilet door.'

She did, and within seconds the security guards arrived and bore Mike away, still yelling abuse at her as he went.

'Annie— Oh, lass, are you all right?' Gideon asked urgently, seeing her slump against the wall.

'Yes— No— I— Oh, Gideon, I've never been so frightened in all my life,' she whispered.

She was trembling all over, and swiftly he half carried, half supported her along to his room.

'Don't move,' he ordered, lowering her into a seat before switching on his kettle and yanking a mug out of the cupboard. 'What the hell was security thinking of? I told them he was banned, that he was never to be allowed up to the wards again.'

'He…he must have got past them somehow,' she murmured through chattering teeth. 'Oh, God, I'm so cold. Why am I so cold, Gideon?'

He abandoned the kettle, knelt in front of her and began chafing her hands between his, but it didn't help. Quickly he pulled his chair round from behind his desk, sat down on it and drew her onto his lap.

'He's gone, Annie—gone,' he said into her hair as she clung to him. 'It's over—all over.'

'I thought…I thought I was going to die,' she said convulsively. 'I thought, he's going to kill me, and there's nothing I can do about it, and Jamie's going to be left with no one to take care of him because David works such long hours, and David doesn't know that Jamie doesn't like carrots or peas, and…'

Shock, her brain dimly registered. Some people retreated into silence. Others couldn't stop talking, and she was obviously one of them.

Gideon didn't seem to mind. In fact, his hold on her tightened so she didn't know whether she was trembling or if he was.

'It's all right,' he said, his voice rough, uneven. 'Nothing can hurt you now. I'm here, and nothing and no one is ever going to hurt you.'

The concern in his voice was the final straw. A sob

came from her, then another, and another, and then she couldn't stop. All the fear she'd felt when Mike had waved that knife at her spilled over, and she buried her face in his chest and sobbed uncontrollably. And he held her, smoothed her hair with his fingers, murmured words she didn't really hear but only knew they were somehow comforting because he was there, and everything was all right.

'I'm sorry, so sorry,' she gasped, when the last of her tears was finally spent. 'You must think I'm so stupid.'

'I think you're brave, and gutsy, and wonderful,' he said huskily, wiping her face gently with his fingers. 'I also think you need something hot to drink,' he added, seeing her shiver.

Quickly he made the coffee, then pressed the mug into her hands.

'I've put sugar in it, and I know you don't normally take sugar, but drink it. It will help.' She tried. She really tried to, but the mug shook so violently in her hands that Gideon had to put his hands over hers to steady them, then guide the mug to her lips. 'Take it slowly,' he ordered as she took a gulp that brought fresh tears to her eyes. 'Take it slowly, one sip at a time.'

She did and, as the warm liquid gradually began to warm her, she managed a tremulous smile. 'That's good. Maybe I should take it with sugar all the time.'

His own lips curved at her poor attempt at a joke, and he touched her cheek gently. 'Better now?'

She nodded. 'What will happen—to Mike?'

'He'll be charged. He has to be, Annie,' he continued as she gazed at him with dismay. 'If we let him away with it, he could come back.'

She shuddered at the thought, and he grasped her shoulders firmly.

'He will never get near you again. I promise.'

Annie believed him. She believed him, and she loved

him, and both thoughts gave her the courage to say, 'Gideon, why have you ignored all my calls?'

His jaw stiffened. 'I don't think this is the time to discuss that. You've just been through a hell of an ordeal—'

'Why, Gideon?' she insisted. 'You don't return my calls, you ignore me at work—'

'Annie—'

'Is it something to do with Nick?' she continued, and saw his jaw set still more. 'I know he's all over me like a rash, but it's not something I want or have encouraged. He seems to think that because he knew me before in Manchester—'

'He's Jamie's father, isn't he?'

Her jaw dropped. How could he have guessed? She was sure she'd never mentioned Nick's name. Never even said he was a gynae consultant.

'Of course he's not,' she said with a desperate attempt at a laugh that sounded false even to her ears. 'I don't know what gave you that idea—'

'My own eyes for a start. It's not a huge resemblance, but it's there, plus the fact you've been behaving like a cat on a hot tin roof ever since he arrived.'

Annie took a gulp of her coffee. It was cold. She was cold again, too. Cold, with a strange icy chill around her heart.

'All right, so he's Jamie's father,' she admitted, 'but that's all he is. He means nothing to me now.'

'Annie, he's Jamie's father, and—' Gideon's eyebrows suddenly snapped down. 'He does know, doesn't he?' She didn't answer, and he swore under his breath. 'Annie, you have to tell him.'

'Why?' she demanded.

'Because the boy's his son,' he protested. 'And he has the right to know that.'

'Nick has *no* rights!' she flared. 'He left me before Jamie was born—'

'Maybe he would have stayed if you'd told him.'

'More likely he'd have run even faster.'

'You don't know that.'

'Gideon, I know Nick a hell of a lot better than you,' she said bitterly, 'and, believe me, if I'd told him I was pregnant I wouldn't have seen him for dust. The man's a jerk, a louse.'

'Is that why you won't go out to dinner with him?'

His eyes were fixed on her, and she gazed back at him in confusion. 'Of course it is. What other reason could there be?'

'I think you're frightened to go out with him,' he said. 'Frightened in case you discover you still love him.'

'That's nonsense.'

'Is it?' He caught her two hands in his, and held onto them tightly. 'Annie, if I were in your shoes I would welcome the opportunity to tell him exactly what I thought of him. To tell him he has a son—a wonderful, beautiful son—that I've raised all by myself with no help wanted or required from him. And then I'd probably sock him.'

'I'm not you.'

'No, you're not, but can you honestly say that you didn't secretly hope this might happen one day? That Nick might come back into your life, divorced, and able to marry you? It would explain why you didn't have a termination—'

'I told you why I didn't have a termination,' Annie protested. 'It had nothing to do with Nick—nothing. He's my past—over, finished. I hoped…' Oh, lord, she couldn't say it. Couldn't say she'd hoped Gideon was her future, not when he was looking at her with an expression she didn't understand. 'Gideon…'

'If Nick really is your past then draw a line under it. Go out with him, tell him about Jamie, and then you really will have closed that chapter of your life.'

'But it *is* closed,' she said in exasperation, wondering how on earth he could possibly be so dense, so blind. 'Going out with Nick wouldn't achieve anything other than to remind me of how stupid I was, of how much he hurt me. And I don't need that, Gideon. I really don't.'

He stared at her silently for a moment, then cleared his throat. 'How long were you and Nick together?'

'What difference does it make?'

'How long, Annie?'

'Six—almost seven months,' she muttered.

'It's a long time to be with someone. A long time to love them. You and I have known each other for what— a month, five weeks?'

'It's not the same, Gideon,' she protested. 'What I feel for you…' There, she'd said it. 'What I feel for you isn't anything like what I felt for Nick.'

'That's what I'm afraid of,' he said bleakly. 'Annie, I want you to be happy—'

'You make me happy,' she protested. 'Gideon, I don't love Nick. I stopped loving him a long time ago.'

'Then prove it. Go out with him. Talk to him. Tell him he's Jamie's father, that he's a rat, and then you can move on with no regrets, no ghosts from your past, no thoughts of what might have been. You owe it to yourself, and to me, to do that.'

She stared up at him blindly. Why couldn't he see that she didn't still love Nick? No way could she still love him. OK, so perhaps he was still the handsomest man she'd ever met, but she was sure—positive—that all she felt for him now was contempt. All right, so maybe when Nick had first left her, before she'd found out about his affair with one of the nurses in Orthopaedics she might have thought—hoped—he would come back, but not afterwards. Definitely not afterwards.

But to go out with him. To sit in a restaurant with him.

To be reminded of things she wanted to forget—had spent four years trying to forget. She couldn't do that, and Gideon couldn't truly love her if he wanted her to.

He was just trying to give her the brush-off. OK, so he'd wrapped it up in a whole load of fancy psychological jargon about burying ghosts and closing chapters, but he was still just trying to give her the brush-off.

She put down her coffee-cup, and got shakily to her feet.

'Thanks for the coffee, and for getting me out of that mess with Louise Harper's boyfriend.'

'Are you going to accept Nick's dinner invitation?' he asked as she walked towards the door.

She turned to face him. 'No.'

'But, Annie—'

'I'd have preferred it if you'd just been honest with me, Gideon,' she said, her face cold, her voice even colder. 'Just told me that you didn't want to go out with me any more.'

'But I do—'

'Enough, Gideon,' she said harshly. 'I don't want to hear any more claptrap from you about closing chapters and burying ghosts. I know how you feel now. You've made it crystal clear.'

She went out of his room without a backward glance, and it took all of Gideon's resolve not to go after her. To pull her into his arms, and kiss her senseless until she'd forgotten she'd ever heard the name Nick Henderson. But he didn't go after her.

If there was the remotest chance that she still felt something for Nick, he had to know. He loved her. He was always going to love her, and he could have played it easy, could have accepted what she'd said without question, but a part of him would always have wondered, just as he suspected a part of her would have wondered, too.

And if she does discover that she still loves this guy? a little voice whispered at the back of his head. What then?

He would live with it, he told himself. He would have to.

CHAPTER TEN

'ARE you quite sure you want to look after Jamie today, David?' Annie asked as she quickly washed the breakfast dishes. 'I mean, it's your day off.'

'And what better way to spend it than by taking my nephew to the Transport Museum?'

'Well, all I can say is you're a glutton for punishment.' She chuckled. 'Once he gets a look at all those old buses, you'll never tear him away.'

'I don't mind. I kind of like them myself.'

'Big kid.' She laughed, then shouted down the corridor, 'Jamie, if you don't hurry up, your Uncle David will go without you.'

A squeal of protest came from Jamie's bedroom, and David grinned. 'I don't think I should have given him that construction kit just yet.'

'Not if you wanted to leave early, you shouldn't,' she said unearthing her hairbrush from down the side of the sofa with relief. 'Now, if I could just find my shoes...'

'You're in Theatre today, aren't you?' David said, holding them out to her. 'Assisting Tom Brooke?'

'That's right.'

'You must be relieved. I mean, it's Nick's last day, and you get to avoid him for half of it.'

'David.'

The warning note in her voice was plain, but he ignored it.

'Look, love, I don't believe any of that crap you gave me about Gideon giving you the brush-off. It's obvious the guy's nuts about you.'

'Then he's got a very funny way of showing it,' she

169

said tightly, wishing for the hundredth time since the weekend that her brother hadn't managed to wheedle the whole sorry story out of her.

'No, he hasn't. In fact, I'd be a bit concerned, too, if the girl I was keen on seemed to be running scared from the man she'd had a child by.'

'I am *not* running scared,' she protested. 'Why can't you and Gideon get it through your thick skulls that I don't feel anything for Nick?'

'It wouldn't surprise me if you still did,' David said, as though she hadn't spoken. 'You and Nick were lovers for what—six, seven months, and he's Jamie's father—'

'David—'

'He's leaving tomorrow, isn't he? So tonight's your last chance to go out with him. I'm afraid I can't babysit for you as I'm on call, but do you think Gideon might do it for you?'

'David, I am not—repeat *not*—going out with Nick Henderson.'

'You could wear that dress I bought you last Christmas—the one you've never worn.'

'Because it's too short, too…too…'

'Exactly.' He nodded. 'It's a stunner, and that's what we want to show Nick. That you're gorgeous, and desirable, and then you can tell him all about Jamie, wipe the floor with him and close that chapter of your life for ever.'

'David—'

'Love, it's like Gideon said. You've got to face your fears because if you don't you'll spend the rest of your life running scared. Always wondering when he might show up again.'

'What's Mummy scared of?' Jamie asked, appearing beside them without warning.

'Where did you spring from, flappy lugs?' David smiled, ruffling his hair.

'What's Mummy scared of?' Jamie pressed, refusing to be diverted.

'The big green dragon who lives in Hyndland, but her friend Gideon is going to kill it for her.'

'There's no such things as dragons,' Jamie said scornfully. 'And even if there was one, Gideon could kill it for sure. I like Gideon. I'd like him to be my daddy.'

'There you go, Annie,' David murmured. 'The menfolk in this family are unanimous.'

'Have you brushed your teeth yet, Jamie?' Annie said, shooting her brother a stern glance.

'Is Gideon going to be my—?'

'Your teeth, Jamie, or no trip with Uncle David,' she said pointedly, and her son scowled, and left the kitchen, dragging his feet.

'Annie—'

'Enough, David,' she said firmly. 'No more talk about Gideon, and I mean it.'

And she did, she thought as she made her way to the hospital. She didn't want to talk about Gideon, and she most certainly didn't want to talk to Nick. All this psychological twaddle her brother and Gideon kept on spouting about ghosts, and fears, and closing chapters. She didn't have any ghosts or fears, but neither did she see the point in opening up old wounds. And that's all she'd be doing if she went out with Nick.

Determinedly she shook her head. All she had to do was to get through today; and tomorrow Nick would be gone. All she had to do was keep her head down and keep out of Nick's way, and tomorrow everything would be back to normal.

And as for Gideon… She would think about what she was going to do about him tomorrow.

'But I'm supposed to be assisting Tom in Theatre,' Annie protested, when Helen gave her the news that Gideon was expecting her on his morning round. 'It's down on the schedule, in black and white.'

'I'm sorry, but ours is not to reason why, et cetera, et cetera,' Helen declared. 'All I know is that Gideon wants you there.'

Like hell he does, Annie thought angrily as the SHO walked away. He's just deliberately throwing me into Nick's company again, and it's not fair. He knows how I feel. He knows I don't want to be anywhere near the man, and if he had any feelings for me at all he wouldn't be doing this.

'All set for another jolly morning jamboree, Annie?' Liz asked, when she saw her.

'Frankly, I'd rather walk over hot coals,' she replied, 'but you'd better give me the update from last night anyway.'

'OK, the good news is Mrs Turner went into labour last night and gave birth to a healthy daughter. Both mother and daughter are doing well, and Mrs Turner's BP seems to have returned to normal.'

'And the bad news?'

'She wants to go home. You'd think she'd realise that having been brought in here with suspected pre-eclampsia, it might be advisable for her to stay with us for a few days to monitor her condition, but with Mrs Turner the light may be on but Mrs Brain is definitely not at home.'

'Too right,' Annie sighed.

'We've also had four new admissions this morning, all scheduled for surgery on Friday. An ovarian cyst, a sterilisation, a possible carcinoma of the cervix and an endometrial carcinoma. I've put their details together in case you want to read them before Gideon arrives.'

'Right.'

A slight frown creased the sister's plump forehead as Annie took the folder from her. 'You OK?'

'Cheesed off would be closer to the truth,' Annie admitted. 'Cheesed off with people giving me advice whether I want it or not. Cheesed off with people trying to run my life for me, instead of letting me live it my way.'

'Whoa, somebody's obviously been rattling your cage, haven't they?' Liz laughed, and a reluctant chuckle sprang from Annie's lips.

'You've got it.' She nodded. 'Have you any brothers, Liz?'

'I'm an only child.'

'Think yourself lucky,' Annie said with feeling.

Quickly she scanned the notes Liz had given her, then glanced down the ward.

So many new faces. So many new women to get to know, and not just their physical symptoms, but what might be worrying them, even frightening them.

'Where's Sylvia Renton?' she asked, seeing the girl's empty bed.

'ICBU,' Liz replied. 'And she went there on her own, with no arm-twisting.'

'You're kidding?' Annie gasped, and Liz shook her head.

'You know how she's been expressing milk for her son but she's always asked me to have it delivered to the intensive care baby unit? Well, this morning she suddenly said she wanted to take it there herself.'

'Oh, I'm so pleased!' Annie exclaimed. 'The hospital psychiatrist must be finally getting through to her.'

'In a pig's eye. It's all the time you've been spending with her, talking to her, reassuring her.'

'I might have helped a bit.'

'A bit?' Liz protested. 'Who brought her in all those books on boys' names and sat discussing them with her until she finally chose one so the poor little soul at least had a name? Who's been taking her down to ICBU every day when she didn't want to go? You're the miracle-worker, Annie.'

'I'm just delighted she's finally beginning to care for Fergus,' Annie said, highly embarrassed by Liz's praise. 'He's such a gorgeous little boy, and I hated the way Sylvia didn't seem interested in him. I know he gave her a really lousy pregnancy, but he's so cute—'

'Hey, you'd better watch out,' Liz said with a chuckle. 'That sounds very much like broody talk to me.'

'No way.' Annie laughed. 'Jamie is more than enough for me, thank you very much, and anyway I'd have to find the right man.'

'I thought you had.'

'Liz.'

'Sorry, I know that particular subject's off limits,' the sister said ruefully as Annie shook her head, 'but I still think it's a crying shame. You and Gideon looked so happy at the Valentine's Ball.'

They had been happy, Annie remembered, but the ball seemed a long time ago now. So much had happened to them since then, so many harsh words had been exchanged, and now she was lonely, so very lonely.

She missed talking to Gideon. She missed his smiles, the way those smiles seemed to make everything all right with the world. But most of all she missed his friendship. OK, so maybe he hadn't talked to her much after Nick had arrived, but these last five days—ever since he'd told her she should go out with Nick—he'd become even more distant and remote, and it hurt. It hurt a lot.

'Whoops, it looks like it's show-time,' Liz said, whipping the scattered pile of magazines off the end of one of the new admission's beds as the door of the ward suddenly swung open and Gideon appeared. 'And wouldn't you know it? Mr Henderson's with him again.'

Of course he was, Annie thought waspishly as Liz hastily explained to their bewildered new admission that she'd get her magazines back after the consultant had left. There was no way Nick would ever have missed his last morning round with them, that she'd known for sure.

Only for today, she thought as she followed Gideon down the ward. I've only got to put up with Nick for one more day, and then he's going to be out of my hair for ever. It sounded good. It sounded marvellous.

'Any problems I should know about, Dr Hart?' Gideon asked.

'Mrs Turner gave birth to a daughter last night, and she wants to discharge herself,' she replied.

Gideon's eyebrows snapped together. 'Doesn't she understand her suspected pre-eclampsia could have been serious?'

'I've tried explaining it to her, so has Liz, but I've a feeling it goes in one ear and out the other.'

'Right,' Gideon said grimly. 'I'll talk to her.'

He did. By the time he was finished there was nothing Mrs Turner didn't know about pre-eclampsia, from it being caused by hypertension and increased fluid in the tissues, to the dangers of it developing into full-blown eclampsia which caused seizures that led to the death of both mother and unborn child.

'But I've had my baby now, Mr Caldwell,' Mrs Turner said complacently, 'so there's no danger of me developing it, is there?'

'No,' Gideon conceded, 'but what I'd like to find out is why you developed it in the first place.'

'Well, I'm afraid I don't have time to lie about in a hospital bed while you find out,' Mrs Turner declared. 'I've four children under the age of ten at home, and they need their mother now.'

'Mrs Turner—'

'Perhaps one of the nurses could bring me the ward phone so I can tell my husband to come and collect me?'

'Mrs Turner, if you discharge yourself against my advice, you'll have to sign a disclaimer, removing all responsibility from us should you become ill,' Gideon declared, clearly keeping his temper with difficulty.

'Fine.' Mrs Turner beamed. 'Now, when can I have the ward phone?'

Gideon turned on his heel and walked away without a word, and Annie hurried after him.

'Isn't there something you can do to stop her?' she said in an urgent undertone. 'She's not in any fit state to go home after just giving birth.'

'Annie, I can't chain her to the bed, and if she's stupid enough to ignore my advice—'

'Mr Caldwell's perfectly right, Annie,' Nick observed as he joined them. 'Some people just won't listen to reason. They bury their heads in the sand, ignore advice—'

'What if the ward phone is busy all day?' Annie said slowly. 'What if so many patients suddenly wanted to use it that it isn't available?'

A slow smile crept across Gideon's cheeks. 'It's sneaky, it's underhanded—I love it. But won't she know it isn't busy?'

'Not if it disappears into the linen cupboard, she won't,' Liz chipped in, overhearing them. 'Of course, we couldn't get away with it for more than a day.'

'Mr Caldwell, this is deeply unethical,' Nick began. 'Denying a patient her rights—'

'Stuff her rights,' Gideon declared succinctly. 'Liz, hide the phone. I'll get onto her husband and see if he can talk some sense into her. If he can't, well…' He shook his head. 'At least we'll have bought her another day in hospital.'

The rest of Gideon's morning round passed without incident. He explained to their four new admissions about the surgery he was going to perform on Friday, answering their questions clearly and concisely, and was just about to leave when, to Annie's embarrassment, Liz told him about Sylvia Renton, and Annie's part in the girl's recovery.

'Well done, Annie,' Gideon said with clear delight. 'Excellent. What we need now is to keep the impetus going, but you've achieved miracles.'

'Annie always was one of the most promising junior doctors I had working under me,' Nick declared, then grinned. 'No *double entendre* meant, of course.'

Like hell there wasn't, Annie thought, feeling her cheeks burn. He just couldn't let it go, could he? He just couldn't stop reminding her of the past.

'If you'd excuse me, Mr Caldwell,' she said, deliberately turning her back on Nick, 'I have paperwork to finish.'

'Not so fast, Annie,' Nick interrupted. 'We never did get round to organising that dinner date, did we? So what about tonight, as it's my last night in Glasgow?'

Gideon's eyes were on her, waiting, watchful, and reluctantly she turned back to Nick.

He was smiling at her, smiling that particular smile which had always made her heart skip a beat, and as she stared back at him she suddenly realised that David and Gideon were right.

She *was* scared. Scared to go out with him. Scared to be alone with him. She'd loved him so much. Had built her entire life round him. And then he'd walked away. For months she'd cried herself to sleep. For months she'd walked around, feeling like only half a person, and then, after Jamie was born, she'd rebuilt her life bit by bit, but always that raw spot had remained. That raw spot of unfinished business, of loose ends needing to be tied up.

Well, they were right, it was time to face her past, she told herself. Time to face her fears. She owed it to Gideon, and to Jamie, but more importantly she owed it to herself to see that he no longer had the power to hurt her.

'Tonight will be just fine,' she managed to say.

'It will?' Nick exclaimed. 'Oh, terrific.'

She didn't know about terrific, but she'd do it.

'You'd better choose the restaurant,' Nick continued. 'I don't know Glasgow at all.'

Somewhere expensive, she thought. Somewhere expensive so that if nothing else it would make a dent in his wallet.

'Stephano's,' she said.

'Stephano's it is.' Nick beamed. 'I'll pick you up at around half seven.'

'Better make it eight,' she said. 'That'll give me time to get home and wash my hair.'

'Eight it is.' He nodded, then swore under his breath as his bleeper went off. 'Sorry, but it looks like Head Office are trying to contact me so I'm afraid I'll have to cut and run. I'll see you tonight, Annie.'

Annie didn't say anything as Nick hurried out of the ward. Neither did Gideon.

'Happy now?' she asked, glancing up at him. 'I'm doing what you wanted me to do, so are you happy now?'

'Yes,' he muttered.

He didn't look happy. In fact, he looked tenser than she'd ever seen him.

'I need a favour,' she said. 'David's on call tonight so would you babysit Jamie for me?'

His jaw dropped. 'You want me to babysit for you?'

'It was your suggestion—this date with Nick—so I think it would be only fair, don't you?'

'What time do you want me to come round?' he said tightly.

'Seven thirty be all right? That should give you and Jamie time to get comfortable together.'

'Seven-thirty it is,' he replied.

'Gideon…'

He didn't answer. He didn't turn round. He just walked away from her without a backward glance.

* * *

But he was bang on time at seven-thirty. She wasn't. She was still wearing her dressing-gown, still drying her hair and still desperately trying to get Jamie to calm down after what had apparently been a fantastic day at the Transport Museum.

'There weren't just buses there, Mummy, but cars, and fire-engines, and delivery vans, and—'

'I know, sweetheart, but Mummy's in a bit of a hurry tonight—'

'Would you like me to entertain him while you get ready?' Gideon suggested as Jamie bounced up and down on the sofa, pretending to be a fire-engine.

'Would you?' she said with relief. 'I'm…I'm a bit harassed tonight.'

And stressed, and panic-stricken, she thought as she shot into her bedroom.

Why had she agreed to this? She should never have agreed to this. It was going to be awful, dreadful. Nick would talk about the past, and she didn't want to talk about the past, and then she'd have to tell him about Jamie, and what if he wasn't horrified, as she suspected he was going to be, but actually thrilled to bits? He and Lucy had never had children, so what if he wanted to play an active part in Jamie's life, and not just in Jamie's, but in hers too?

'Stop crossing bridges before you get to them,' she told herself aloud as she finished drying her hair, then put on her make-up with a shaking hand. 'Stop panicking before you have to.'

It was easier said than done, she thought as she slipped into her dress. A hell of a lot easier.

'Is…is that what you're wearing?' Gideon said, visibly shaken as she walked into the sitting room.

In truth, she'd thought the dress was awful, too, when David had given it to her last Christmas. He'd called it a little black dress, and while it was certainly black it was also very little. In fact, there wasn't nearly enough of it. Ending halfway up her thighs, hugging every inch of her body, with only minuscule shoestring straps to prevent it from falling off, she felt like an over-exposed idiot, but there was no way she was going to go to a place like Stephano's in a checked skirt and sweater.

'David gave it to me as a present,' she said defensively.

'David would.'

'You don't like it.'

'If I were going out with you I'd probably love it, but, no, I can't say I'm happy at the thought of you wearing that to go out with Nick.'

Was he jealous? She hoped very much that he was, but she didn't have time to ask. Not when her doorbell was ringing.

'Wow, but you look sensational, Annie!' Nick exclaimed as she let him in. 'In fact, not just sensational, but…' He came to a halt in the sitting room doorway. 'Mr Caldwell, I didn't expect to see you here.'

Gideon smiled. 'I'm moonlighting. With what the NHS pay me, I have to do babysitting at night to make ends meet.'

Nick gave him a hard stare, then clearly decided to ignore him. 'Are you ready, Annie?'

'Who's that man?' Jamie frowned, staring at Nick.

'A friend of Mummy's, sweetheart. Now, you're to go to bed when Gideon says. No tantrums, or trying to stay up late, OK?'

She might as well have been talking to the wall. Jamie was already in deep discussion with Gideon about the construction kit David had given him that morning.

'I'm going, if anybody's interested,' she said.

Gideon at least managed a perfunctory wave in her direction, and she didn't know whether to be angry or amused as she allowed Nick to escort her out of her flat.

'I didn't know you had a kid,' Nick said when they'd reached his hired car.

'Oh, there's a lot you don't know about me,' she said cryptically, 'but that's what this evening's all about, isn't it? Catching up on old times, telling each other what we've been doing for the last four years.'

They did. Or, to be more accurate, Nick did. Once they'd arrived at the restaurant and had ordered their meal, he told her all about his new job, what a great honour it had been to be selected and how it was undoubtedly going to lead on to bigger and greater things.

He used to do that in the past, she remembered as she sat in silence opposite him. Talk about himself all the time. She'd been fascinated back then. Fascinated and impressed by the people he'd known, the places he'd gone, the places he intended going, but now...

She wondered how Gideon was getting on with Jamie. Unconsciously her lips curved. Heaven knew, her son was no angel, and though he and Gideon had got on well together in the park she wouldn't put it past him to play up tonight, refuse to go to bed and throw a gigantic tantrum.

'So what have you been doing for these past four years since you left the Manchester Infirmary?' Nick eventually asked, when the waiter had brought them their tagliatelle carbonara. 'I know you have a son, but what else have you been doing?'

'There's not actually a lot you can do when you're a single parent,' she replied. 'In fact, this job at the Belfield is the first I've had since Jamie was born.'

'That's bound to affect your career prospects,' Nick said. 'I mean, taking time out is bad enough, but having a kid... Promotion boards tend to regard it as insufficient commitment.'

She nodded, and cleared her throat. 'When you met Jamie, did he remind you of anybody?'

'I can't say I paid much attention to him.' Nick smiled

apologetically. 'One kid generally looks very much like another to me.'

She gritted her teeth, picked up her handbag and produced a photograph. 'Look at this—refresh your memory.'

Nick stared down at the photograph, then handed it back. 'Sorry, but, like I said, one kid looks pretty much like another to me.'

'He's your son.'

He stared at her speechlessly for a second, then his lips curved into an uncertain smile. 'This is a wind-up—right—a joke?'

She shook her head. 'No wind-up. No joke.'

'Then how come you never told me about him before?' he demanded. 'He must be at least four, if not five, so it's a bit late in the day for you to try to palm him off as mine, especially as you left the Manchester Infirmary three months after we split up.'

'After you dumped me, you mean,' she retorted. 'I left the Infirmary because I was five months pregnant.'

'You told me you were on the pill.'

'And as an obs and gynae consultant, you should know that the pill isn't a hundred per cent effective.'

'That kid could be anybody's,' Nick said scornfully. 'You weren't living with me when we were an item, so he could be anybody's.'

Contempt welled inside her. Contempt for him, and contempt for herself for ever having fallen in love with him in the first place.

'You're a poor excuse for a man, aren't you?' she said.

Anger darkened his cheeks, then he delved into his pocket and extracted his wallet.

'OK, how much?'

'What?' she said in confusion.

'I presume this meal is just a means of squeezing some cash from me, so how much do you want?'

How could she ever have thought she loved this man? she wondered as she stared at him. How could she have been scared to go out with him? He was nothing. Less than nothing.

'I wouldn't take a penny from you, Nick,' she said, her voice ice-cold. 'A friend said I should tell you about Jamie, and now that I have I'm going. I'd like to say it's been nice meeting you again, but it hasn't.'

Annie rose to her feet, and he put out a hand to stay her.

'Set your sights on Gideon Caldwell now, have you?' he sneered. 'Well, you always did have a thing about consultants, didn't you?'

'That's right.' She nodded. 'And that's why I can't possibly go without leaving you with something to remember me by.'

And with a smile on her lips, she lifted her plate of tagliatelle carbonara and emptied the contents over his head.

'Is there something wrong with your food, madam?' the manager asked with concern when she retrieved her coat from beside his desk.

'The food was lovely, thank you.' She smiled. 'It was the company that was the problem.'

The manager glanced out into the restaurant where Nick was involved in a heated argument with one of the waiters who was trying to remove the tagliatelle from his hair, and his lips quirked. 'I see. Would madam like me to get her a taxi?'

Why not? she thought. OK, so it would be expensive, but the quicker she got home, the better.

Annie let herself in as quietly as she could, reasoning that Jamie was bound to be in bed, but he wasn't. Both he and Gideon were fast asleep on the sofa, and a chuckle sprang to her lips. Gideon had clearly had a stressful evening.

Toys were strewn around the floor, the TV was on and the construction kit David had given Jamie was still in bits.

Carefully she turned off the television so as not to wake either of them, but years of medicine meant Gideon slept very lightly and his eyes immediately fluttered open.

'Hi, there,' he murmured, his lips curving into a gentle smile.

'Hi, there, yourself.' She smiled back. 'Rough evening?'

'You could say that.' A slight frown creased his forehead. 'I didn't hear Nick's car.'

'I came back by taxi.'

His eyes shot to the clock on the mantelpiece, and the frown on his forehead deepened. 'But it's not even ten o'clock. What happened? Annie, did that bastard—?'

She put her fingers to his lips quickly. 'Let me put Jamie to bed, and then I'll explain.'

Gently she eased Jamie off his chest and carried him through to his bed. He was dead to the world, and it didn't take long to get him into his pyjamas and into bed, but it was clearly too long for Gideon because he whirled round impatiently as soon as she came back to the sitting room.

'OK, what happened?' he demanded without preamble.

'You were right,' she said, sitting down on the sofa. 'I did have some old ghosts, some demons.'

He nodded slowly. 'And have you…?' He paused. 'Have you laid them to rest, or…?'

She smiled. 'Come and sit down, and I'll tell you exactly what happened.'

And she told him. She told him everything Nick had said, and about the plate of tagliatelle.

'Lord, but I wish I'd been there,' Gideon exclaimed, wiping the tears of laughter from his eyes with the back of his hand. 'I'd have given a month's salary to see Nick's face, and the faces of the other diners when you upended that plate. The restaurant was busy, I hope?'

Her lips quirked. 'There wasn't a spare table.'

'Perfect.' He grinned, then his smile became a little lopsided. 'I didn't want to do that, you know—practically force you go out with Nick—but I thought for your own sake…'

'I know.' She nodded. 'So what now, Gideon? I've done what you asked—faced my fears. What happens now?'

He reached out and caught her hand in his, his face suddenly unsure, uncertain. 'Annie, I know I'm not Jamie's father, but I love your son as much as if he were my own.'

'He told me this morning that he'd like you to be his daddy.'

'Did he?'

'Yes, he did.'

'Then do you think…?' He stared down at her hand and began to awkwardly twist the single ring she wore on her right hand between his fingers. 'Do you think it would matter to him eventually that I wasn't his real father?'

'Gideon, some anonymous donor to a sperm bank would be as much of a father to Jamie as Nick has been, or ever wants to be.'

'And what about you?' he asked.

She couldn't resist it. 'Well, I don't actually want a daddy.'

'Annie, you know what I mean,' he protested. 'Could you…? Do you think you could ever love me enough to contemplate spending the rest of your life with me?'

His hair was sticking up all over the place as though he and Jamie had been playing some pretty energetic games, and she stretched up and smoothed it down. 'Oh, Gideon, don't you know even now how much I love you?'

'I'd like to think that you do, but Nick... He's everything I'm not...'

'I don't want you to be like Nick,' she protested. 'I want you to stay exactly the way you are because I love you, you big idiot.'

'You do?'

'Uh-huh. After tonight I know with absolute certainty that you're everything I always wanted. Everything I thought I'd never have.'

'Oh, lass.' He kissed her long and hard, then drew her into his arms and held her tight. 'I wish I'd been born ten centuries ago. I could have got out my sword, fought him for you.'

'Slapped your gauntlet across his face, then demanded a duel at dawn?' she said with a bubble of laughter.

Gideon's lips quirked ruefully. 'Something like that. Then I'd be sure you'd never have any regrets.'

'Gideon, if I had any regrets I wouldn't be sitting here with you, and Nick wouldn't be putting his suit into the dry-cleaner's.'

'It looks like it's official, then,' he said, 'apart from one very important thing.'

'What thing?' she questioned.

'You haven't said you'll marry me.'

'You haven't asked me,' she pointed out.

'Do you want the full down-on-my-knees bit?' he asked, his brown eyes dancing, 'or will you take pity on a poor old man who's had a very long day, and an even longer night, trying to entertain your son?'

Annie chuckled. 'I think we can skip the knees bit.'

'Hallelujah for that,' he said with feeling. 'Annie Hart, will you marry me, be my wife, look after me in my old age, and love me to bits in the meantime?'

'Should I hum and haw a bit here, do you think?' she asked, her own eyes sparkling. 'I mean, if you're my knight in shining armour, maybe I should play the coy maiden for a while.'

'You'd never get away with it—not wearing that dress,' he growled. 'Just put me out of my misery, woman. Will you marry me?'

She smiled. 'Whenever you want, Sir Gideon.'

Modern Romance™
...seduction and
passion guaranteed

Tender Romance™
...love affairs that
last a lifetime

Sensual Romance™
...sassy, sexy and
seductive

Blaze Romance™
...the temperature's
rising

Medical Romance™
...medical drama on
the pulse

Historical Romance™
...rich, vivid and
passionate

27 new titles every month.

*With all kinds of Romance for
every kind of mood...*

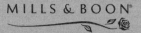

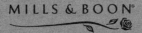

MILLS & BOON®

Medical Romance™

DR MICHAELIS'S SECRET by Margaret Barker

An emergency rescue on Ceres Island has recent
arrival Staff Nurse Sara Metcalfe working with local
doctor Michaelis Stangos – and from the moment she
sees him diving into the waves she's hooked. But
Sarah senses he's hiding a painful secret. A secret
that's holding him back from what could be a perfect
relationship...

THE FAMILY PRACTITIONER by Leah Martyn

Life is pretty uneventful for Joanne, working at the
local clinic – until her teenage son Jason comes home
with an outrageous request that sends Joanna
marching off to see just what Dr Matthew McKellar is
up to! Suddenly her life is in chaos. She's got a
new job, with Matt as her new boss – and as her
new lover...

HER CONSULTANT BOSS by Joanna Neil

Dr Megan Llewellyn couldn't work out what she felt
most for her boss, consultant Sam Benedict –
exasperation or desire! Was he hiding an attraction
to her that was as intense as hers for him? When a
fire destroyed her home and Megan found herself
living with Sam she quickly found her answer!

On sale 7th February 2003

*Available at most branches of WH Smith,
Tesco, Martins, Borders, Eason, Sainsbury's
and all good paperback bookshops.* 0103/03b

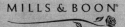

2 FREE

books and a surprise gift!

We would like to take this opportunity to thank you for reading this Mills & Boon® book by offering you the chance to take TWO more specially selected titles from the Medical Romance™ series absolutely FREE! We're also making this offer to introduce you to the benefits of the Reader Service™—

- ★ FREE home delivery
- ★ FREE gifts and competitions
- ★ FREE monthly Newsletter
- ★ Exclusive Reader Service discount
- ★ Books available before they're in the shops

Accepting these FREE books and gift places you under no obligation to buy, you may cancel at any time, even after receiving your free shipment. Simply complete your details below and return the entire page to the address below. *You don't even need a stamp!*

YES! Please send me 2 free Medical Romance books and a surprise gift. I understand that unless you hear from me, I will receive 4 superb new titles every month for just £2.55 each, postage and packing free. I am under no obligation to purchase any books and may cancel my subscription at any time. The free books and gift will be mine to keep in any case.

M3ZEA

Ms/Mrs/Miss/Mr ....Initials......................................
BLOCK CAPITALS PLEASE

Surname ....

Address ....

....

....Postcode...............................

Send this whole page to:
UK: FREEPOST CN81, Croydon, CR9 3WZ
EIRE: PO Box 4546, Kilcock, County Kildare (stamp required)

Offer valid in UK and Eire only and not available to current Reader Service subscribers to this series. We reserve the right to refuse an application and applicants must be aged 18 years or over. Only one application per household. Terms and prices subject to change without notice. Offer expires 30th April 2003. As a result of this application, you may receive offers from Harlequin Mills & Boon and other carefully selected companies. If you would prefer not to share in this opportunity please write to The Data Manager at the address above.

Mills & Boon® is a registered trademark owned by Harlequin Mills & Boon Limited.
Medical Romance™ is being used as a trademark.